# THE INFERNAL CIRCLE

# OF ETERNAL RETURN

By the same author

The End of Everything We Know

**The Infernal Circle of Eternal Return**
Aaron Harvie

Cover Art, Design & Layout by
Blood, Brains & Aliens &
Andy Thai

Edited by
Karen Lateo

The Infernal Circle of Eternal Return.
By Aaron Harvie.

All Rights Reserved
ISBN 978-0-6457669-3-6
First published in 2025
© Aaron Harvie 2025 1st Edition.

This is a work of fiction. Names, characters, businesses,
places, events, locales and incidents are either the product
of the author's imagination or used in a fictitious manner.
Any resemblance to actual persons, living or dead, or actual
events is purely coincidental.

Edited by Karen Lateo.

For April... you know why

*This life, as you now live it and have lived it, you will have to live once moreand innumerable times more; and there will be nothing new in it, but every pain and every joy and every thought and sigh... The eternal hourglass of existence is turned over again and again — and you with it, speck of dust!*

**Friedrich Nietzsche, 1882.**

1976

**7.10 am: Brady Hitchcock's apartment.**

The blare of the alarm clock cut through the fog of Brady's hangover like a buzzsaw. He woke with a start, for one endless moment unsure what day it was, who he was, or even where he was sleeping.

Then it came flooding back and he groaned loudly.

As if sensing he was about to roll over and go back to sleep, the alarm clock crackled at him impatiently, the static pure agony in his tender brain.

"Alright, alright. Jesus fucking Christ," he groaned as he cracked open a bloodshot eye and peered blearily over the bedside table. "What time is it?"

The flip cards taunted him: 7.11 am.

With some effort, he reached over and slammed his hand down on the top of the alarm, accidently hitting snooze.

Still, it was quiet, which was good enough for Brady.

He sat up slowly and ignored the ruin of his head. It screamed loudly in protest as he swung his legs out from beneath the covers, planting his feet on the hardwood floor.

It was cold, really cold.

And his bedroom was a disaster.

It looked like the room of some pimply faced shit in a fraternity, not the room of a decorated police sergeant in his forties. The bedside and the floor were littered with empty beer cans, dirty clothes, and a quarter-filled bottle of some cheap rot-gut vodka. A framed family portrait of Brady and his ex-wife with their two kids had the remnants of an 8-ball of coke spilled across the glass.

As Brady tried to stand, his stomach lurched. A wave of sick rolled over him. He felt his complexion sallow as saliva flooded his mouth and cold beads of sweat pearled on his forehead. He sat back on the bed, breathed deep and felt around blindly for the bottle, scared to drop his head too low for fear of throwing up on the floor.

His alcoholic hands were shaking.

When he found the bottle, he expertly twisted off the cap, sending it spinning to the floor like a top. He swallowed deeply. The warm wave crashed over him almost immediately and he swallowed again, then one more time, finishing most of the vodka. Like a cold shadow retreating from the sunlight, he felt the sickness and his shakes start to melt away. The grey light streaming into the room through the tiny window above his dresser started to take on a diffused, golden hue.

It was only then that he noticed there was a woman asleep in the bed beside him.

It took him a moment to process that there was another person in the room.

He couldn't remember last night. There was not even the flash of a memory in his brain, just the blackness of beers, vodka, coke, smack, Quaaludes and whatever the fuck else he'd taken. And even though he'd been separated from his wife for almost a year, he still felt an overwhelming wave of guilt and shame, like he was some little kid about to be scolded in school.

"Hey. Uh, hello... are you awake?"

Brady reached over and shook her.

She rolled to face him, blinking away sleep from her dusty eyes, and smiled.

"Mm... good morning."

"Hi," he replied.

She ignored his rude tone and stretched seductively across the bed, letting the sheets slip down across her naked body.

"It's so early," she smiled invitingly. "Why don't you come back to bed?"

For some reason this pissed him off, and he regarded her coldly. The sag of her overly large breasts. The acne on her forehead and chin. The dark regrowth on her cheap, yellow-banded dye job.

"What's your name again?"

Her face crumpled and she sat up, suddenly feeling vulnerable and used, pulling the sheets over her naked chest as if to protect herself.

"It's Sheila. We met at the Gemini Lounge last night..." she stopped for a beat, waiting for him to catch up. When he didn't, she continued, "I can't believe you don't even remember my name."

She looked at him as though she'd been violated.

"Look, don't make a big fucking deal out of this, okay? I was drunk, I don't remember what happened last night, honest."

She looked at him, outraged and hurt, searching for the faintest semblance of a decent person in his eyes.

"I gotta get out of here, I gotta go to work..."

She nodded, giving him the benefit of the doubt. Maybe he wasn't an asshole, she thought. Maybe he was just being straight with her.

She dropped her guard.

"Yeah, all right, just give me a minute."

Shelia got out of bed, pulling the sheet with her for modesty, as she began to scoop her underwear and clothes off the floor. She dressed, turning her back to him till she had hooked her bra. Even though they'd been intimate last night, she felt anything but comfortable in the cold light of day.

She stepped into her dress and pulled it up over her shoulders and said, as casually as she could, "You know, I don't start till nine tonight. Maybe if you're not busy we could get some dinner or something?"

He didn't miss a beat.

"Look, I don't wanna be rude or nothing... How about I just see you at the bar sometime?"

Her complexion flushed scarlet. Tears of anger and embarrassment welled in her eyes, as hope ignited into outrage and humiliation.

"You fucking prick." That was all she could say.

Brady's eyes were as cold as a shark's. "Just calm down alright, there's no reason to get angry."

His absolute indifference was the final straw and she saw red, her rage matching the degradation she felt. Shelia threw her shoes on the floor and rushed at Brady, lunging across the bed, lashing at his face with her nails like some wild cat.

She missed, scratching his forearm as she sprawled across the bed.

He stepped back in shock, cradling his arm for a moment in surprise, before snarling at her and shouting.

"Jesus... are you crazy or something? Get your shit and get out of here before I kick your fucking ass."

Shelia screamed at him in humiliation and scrambled off the bed, grabbing her shoes from the floor as she ran for the door.

"You can't treat people like this..."

She stopped, her face smeared with tears and mascara, and looked back at him.

"You're a fucking asshole, you know that?"

This pushed Brady over the edge. He stooped down and retrieved the vodka bottle from the floor, threatening to throw it.

"Get the fuck out of here."

When she didn't move, he lobbed it at the wall near the doorjamb. It shattered into a million pieces.

She ran from the apartment, slamming the door behind her.

"Don't you ever fucking speak to me again!" was the last thing she said.

Brady stood beside his bed breathing heavily, his heart pounding in his chest.

"Fuck her," he said out loud to himself.

But it came out meek. Like he was ashamed. Like he knew he was the piece of shit she said he was.

Brady fished a cigarette out of the packet on the bedside table and lit up, drawing deeply and exhaling with a coughing fit. He didn't feel like himself anymore. He felt like he was watching himself in a movie...

Then the phone rang.

Brady snapped back and got up, answering it on the third ring.

"Hello?"

"Brady, is that you?"

It was his Captain. Captain Frank Dodd. Brady had worked for him for almost 15 years.

"Yeah, Captain."

"Jesus, you sound like shit."

Brady smiled at this.

"I'm alright. Think I gotta cold or something."

There was a brief pause before Captain Frank Dodd continued, almost as if he knew exactly what Brady was up to but was choosing to ignore it.

"Yeah, okay Brady, if you say so. Look, we gotta call about twenty minutes ago. Another girl went missing last night. Looks like our killer's back again."

Brady felt the rest of the world suddenly slip away. His hangover. The stupid fight with Shelia. His family.

Everything.

Suddenly he felt focused.

"Shit. Okay, what do we know?"

"Not much. All Metro officers have been called in to help. Your partner is on his way to pick you up now."

Brady looked around the room. He was naked; his arm had a welt from where Shelia had scratched him.

"Right now? I mean Captain, I…"

Dodd cut him off.

"Just pull yourself together. You got fifteen minutes."

The line went dead before Brady could say another thing.

Fifteen minutes wasn't long.

He showered then dressed, choosing the cleanest outfit he could find on the floor. Next, he cut two long logs of coke and snorted them, washing them down with a beer before heading out the door.

**7.32 am: Detective Ted Rankin's sedan.**

Brady Hitchcock pushed open the dented double doors of his apartment building. He walked outside to the grey, dreary street, just as his partner's shitty brown Ford pulled up to the kerb. It was bitterly cold, and Brady felt his nose run as his breath plumed from his mouth. He wiped the snot with the back of his hand, then popped the collar of his brown leather coat as he crossed the street.

"Morning Sergeant," Detective Ted Rankin smiled as he got into the car.

It reeked of Rankin's cheap cologne, the alpine-fresh stink curling Brady's nostrils.

He regarded his partner with contempt and remained silent, choosing to ignore his pleasantries and light a cigarette instead. Ted Rankin took his partner's rudeness in his stride and pulled out from the kerb, heading south.

The car quickly filled with acrid blue smoke. The pair sat in silence, until Rankin coughed uncomfortably.

"You mind opening your window, Sarge?"

Brady shook his head with disdain and glared at Rankin as he rolled the window down a crack.

He'd never liked Detective Rankin, not since he was part-nered with him a year ago. Brady thought he was a douche-bag; a fucking show-off with perfectly blow-waved hair. He wore fucking sneakers and flared jeans – for Christ's sake, what kind of cop wore sneakers on the job? And that fucking brown-nosing, at-risk youth outreach program he ran to impress the brass made him want to puke.

No one was buying it.

Least of all Brady.

He snorted, as if simply thinking about Detective Rankin gave him a bad taste in his mouth. Brady retrieved his silver hip flask from his inside jacket pocket and looked at Rankin as he drank, challenging him to say something.

Rankin frowned disapprovingly but remained tight-lipped, his eyes on the road.

"You got a problem?"

"No problem, Sergeant."

Brady chuckled to himself and stared at his partner.

"Yeah, you do. I can't stand this fucking passive-aggressive shit, you hear me Detective?"

Rankin kept his eyes on the road and said nothing as Brady continued to glare at him.

"I get a fucking lifetime of this shit from my ex-wife already."

Brady took a long draw from his cigarette.

"I dunno, I mean, it's not even eight o'clock in the morning..." Rankin hesitated.

"What the fuck do you care?"

"I just think we got a job to do is all. Another girl's gone missing... it's probably not gonna help too much if you're drinking on the job."

This piqued Brady's interest.

"Is that so?"

"I mean, I don't think the captain would be too happy if he knew you were drinking on the job."

If Brady wasn't angry already, he was fucking furious now.

"Really? And who's going to tell him, you?"

"No."

"Just in case you forgot detective, I've been an officer here in Port Perte since '54. That's twenty-two years on the force, shitbag. I've been a fucking sergeant here in Metro for the past nine. When did you transfer in, a year ago?"

Rankin gripped the wheel tight, regretting he'd even opened his mouth.

"Eighteen months, sir."

Brady leaned in close, barely containing his seething fury.

"Fucking know-it-all rookie," Brady snarled. "Get this through your head, okay. I'm the big fucking fish in this pond. You're just a fucking turd floating in a bowl. You even think about going to the captain and I'll personally see that you're busted down to uniform and doing paperwork till you're blind, you got that?

Rankin kept his eyes on the road and nodded. "Yeah, I got it."

"Good. Then shut up and drive the fucking car."

## 7.46 am: The EZ Mart.

The EZ Mart convenience store was on the corner of Broad
Street and Meadow Avenue. It was a modest brown brick
building with a flat roof and large glass windows. Out the
front was a five-car carpark, the asphalt strewn with leaves
from the tall trees that lined the street. Normally the store
glowed brightly day and night with cheerful fluorescent lights
and a gawdy blinking sign out front. But today it was shut
up and dark. There was something very off- putting about it.
Even the colourful promotional posters for hamburgers and
ice-cream and soft drinks plastered across the façade looked
sad and hopeless.

Brady got out of the car.

You could feel the violence in the air, as if the horror that
had played out earlier had somehow permeated everything
around it. Brady could taste something bitter, almost metallic,
as if the air itself had been tainted. He noticed with disgust
that a large group of onlookers was already crowding around
the police lines.

Brady made his way past the police cars parked on the street
and roughly pushed through the crowd, ducking under the
crime scene tape and barking at the first uniform he could
find.

"Alright, what have we got?"

A lanky young officer smiled and made his way over towards
him. He had an Adam's apple that looked like he'd tried to
swallow a tennis ball.

"Good morning, Sergeant," the officer said, way too eagerly.

Brady hated uniforms. They always fucked everything up.

"What's your name?"

"Officer Dailey, sir."

"Get me up to speed."

"Yes sir. Uh, well, I think, that is, we think this could be the Monster again."

This pissed Brady off. He'd been on this case for almost a year. This fucking idiot didn't have a clue who the Monster was.

"Don't tell me what you think, tell me what you know. You got an ID on the victim?"

"Sorry Sergeant. The victim is Abby Robbins, aged fourteen. She lives a few blocks away on Meadow Avenue. Owner of the store says she came in just before he closed, around ten o'clock last night, to buy her mother some cigarettes. No one's seen her since. Her parents reported her missing just before midnight."

"Anybody see anything?"

"No sir. We're canvassing the area for witnesses as we speak."

"Good, did you notify the parents?"

"We're on it now, sir."

"Alright. Keep me posted."

Brady surveyed the crime scene. It was ugly. Cops milled

around here and there, talking, wasting time. Down the far-right corner of the carpark, Brady could see the police crime scene photographer Steve Gilmore and the county forensic pathologist Dr Amanda Pyke huddled around something on the ground. Nearby, a lone red child's sneaker lay on its side, next to two sets of tyre tracks.

Brady motioned for Rankin to follow him as he crossed the lot towards them.

Gilmore and Pyke both looked up and mumbled hello. Their mood was grim and neither looked overly happy to see him. A small, severed finger was curled up in a dried puddle of blood on the asphalt between them.

"Is it the same as the others?" Brady asked.

Dr Pyke looked up at him coldly and nodded. They'd had a thing when he was still married, and it had ended badly.

"I'm afraid so. Injuries look consistent with the other Monster victims. Judging by the lividity, I'd say she was attacked about eight to ten hours ago, which fits the timeline."

"That's a fucked-up calling card," Rankin muttered grimly.

Brady took a deep breath and closed his eyes for a moment, as his hangover crashed down upon his head in a wave of pain and nausea.

"My fucking head's pounding. Anyone got any aspirin?"

They all shook their heads.

Brady knelt gingerly, peering at the little girl's finger. It was shrivelled and blue and didn't look real. The flesh at the base of the digit had been stripped back up to the knuckle and the bone beneath had snapped and splintered like a green stick. Then he noticed the fingernail was painted with cheap glitter nail polish.

It was the same kind his daughter used.

Brady could taste the sour sting of bile rise up in his throat. He stood up and looked out across the lot.

"Steve, you get pictures of those tyre tracks over there?"

The photographer glanced over at where Brady was looking.

"Not yet."

"Make sure you do. If they're from our suspect's car this might be the first break we've had in the case."

Just then, Abby Robbins' parents arrived at the crime scene. It was tragic. The girl's mother was hysterical, her face a mess of pain and tears and mascara. Her husband looked like a shell, almost catatonic. All he could do was hold his wife close and keep her from collapsing on the street.

Brady couldn't deal with this shit. He wasn't up for grieving fucking parents. Not this morning.

"Jesus Christ, this is all I fucking need. I thought that dipshit uniform was taking care of the parents."

The uniforms around the line closed in as Abby's mother tried to push her way past the line, franticly screaming her daughter's name.

"My fucking hangover's too bad to deal with this shit today," Brady turned and looked back at Dr Pyke. "Let's get that finger packed up and back to the lab. When can I come and see you?"

"Around noon," she replied robotically.

Before Brady could respond, Officer Dailey called out to him from across the lot.

"Sergeant Hitchcock, sir."

"What now?" Brady growled to himself.

Officer Dailey trotted over, a big, goofy smile plastered across his face.

"Sergeant, we just got word from Captain Dodd over the radio. He needs you back at the station ASAP."

"Tell him I'm busy."

"He said you'd say that. He told me to tell you the State Police are coming in for a briefing on the case at nine, and if you aren't there you should go find yourself another job."

He shook his head and snorted in frustration. "When it rains it fucking pours."

Rankin chimed in.

"I'll go take care of the parents, boss. You go see the captain and I'll meet you at the station later."

For the first time ever, Brady didn't spit back his reply.

"Yeah, that's a good idea. While you're there, go bag that girl's shoe before the parents see it. Best not add to their fucking misery, okay?"

Rankin nodded yes and started towards the red shoe.

Brady turned his attention to the uniformed officer standing before him, struggling remember his name.

"You, whatever your fucking name is..."

"It's Officer Dailey sir."

"Like it matters. Make yourself useful and go get me a fucking ride to the station – now!"

**9.05 am: Port Perte Metro Police Station.**

The briefing room of the Metro Police station was lit by a bank of overhead fluorescent tubes that cast a cold, harsh light across the linoleum floor and fake-wood-panelled walls. In the centre of the room was a long conference table. Seated in the plastic moulded chairs around it were members of the State Police command, the Mayor and the Chief of Police, as well as other ranking officers in the department. Brady stood at the lectern at the far end, a hastily compiled board of gruesome crime-scene photos and evidence behind him.

"Okay, Captain Dodd has asked me to give you an update on the case," Brady said as he slurped a cup of scalding-hot coffee, hoping to get rid of his hangover. He cursed quietly to himself for not having another line before coming in to give the briefing. "As you all know, we've had an incident this morning and time is a factor, so I'll keep this short. In the last fourteen months, two teenage girls have been abducted and murdered in Port Perte: Margaret Rose, aged fourteen, and Raynor Langton, twelve. Both are suspected to be victims of the same offender."

The captain of the State Police, a horrible fuck named Shay Dalton, fidgeted in his chair, then interrupted.

"Where did the name come from, Sergeant? The one the press is using?"

"What? The Monster?"

"Yeah, that's the one."

"Well sir, the press gave our perp the name after some of the more confronting details of the second murder were leaked."

A few of the brass cleared their throats and shifted uncomfortably at the mention of the leak. Brady waited for them to settle before he continued.

"The killer's MO is pretty consistent in both cases. The victims were all taken from public places. There were reports of witnesses seeing a dark-coloured sedan in the area prior to all three abductions, and tyre tracks found at the scene confirm that a vehicle was involved. But at this point, we still haven't been able to confirm make or model. In both cases, the killer bit off the victim's right index finger and left it at the site of the abduction, like a calling card. Their bodies were discovered no more than 24 hours after they went missing. In both cases we received an anonymous phone call from someone we suspect to be the killer, telling us they'd committed the murder."

Police Chief Greaves was next to chime in.

"Do you have a recording of these calls?"

"No sir."

Brady cleared his throat before he continued.

"The victims were found in black plastic garbage bags, dumped in waterways. They were both dismembered, and their heads mutilated."

Mayor Finn glanced over at his chief of police in concern. "What exactly does that mean, Sergeant?"

"The killer removed the head, arms and legs. Both girls had their eyes, ears and tongues removed, and then their eyelids, ear canals and mouths sewn shut. At this stage, we haven't recovered the missing organs."

The room erupted in outrage.

"Please tell me these wounds happened post-mortem," prompted Mayor Finn.

Brady couldn't muster the right response. Instead, he sounded like a robot.

"From what we can tell, the victims were alive for at least part of the mutilation."

It was several moments more before the room settled down and Brady could talk again.

"Although there has been no evidence of sexual assault in either case, we have been able to determine that the offender has type-O blood, lifted from saliva samples found on both victims' severed fingers. We have no fingerprints. No hair or fibre evidence. No witnesses, motives or connection with the victims."

"Jesus fucking Christ," someone said.

Brady felt the room turn against him. The reaction was primal, like a mob trying to find someone to punish for a crime, whether they were guilty or not.

"And as of this morning there's another one. Is that right, Sergeant?"

All eyes were on him.

"We believe so, yes."

He may as well have abducted the girl himself.

"Given our killer's history, come 10 o'clock tonight, we've officially got a serial killer on our hands," Police Chief Greaves stated, a grim tone in his voice.

Even though he knew he should keep his mouth shut, Brady couldn't help correcting him.

"Well not exactly, sir. There is one more case."

Police Chief Greaves sat up straight in his chair, as if he couldn't believe what he was hearing.

"Another one? How come I'm only hearing this now?"

Brady could feel Captain Dodd glaring at him from across the room, his eyes drilling into his skull.

And, as stupid as it was, he kept on talking.

"Well sir, it's not official. We got a call a couple of months ago, very similar to the other two calls from the killer, only in this case there was no severed finger or body recovered. We're unsure if this was genuine contact from our perp or a prank. We're currently checking it against missing persons cases but at this point we don't have much more to go on."

"So, you're saying there could be more of these?"

Police Chief Greaves glanced across the table in concern.

"We don't know. But at this stage we're not ruling it out."

Police Chief Greaves got to his feet and straightened his jacket. His eyes blazed with fury.

"Thank you, Sergeant. That will be all. Captain Dodd, we'd like to speak to you in your office, now."

The brass filed out of the briefing room and into the captain's office.

Brady lit a cigarette and watched them go. The conversation inside looked heated. This wasn't good. Any idiot could see that.

He moved closer, near the door, hoping to hear what was being said. Ted Rankin strolled into the bullpen eating a doughnut, a wide smile plastered across his face. Brady could feel his contempt rise just at the sight of him. He hated the whole easy-going, congenial vibe Rankin had.

In fact, he hated Ted Rankin, period.

"How'd it go?" Rankin asked.

"Not good. Did you get anything else from the scene?"

"Parents say Abby Robbins left their house at quarter to ten with strict instructions to go to the EZ Mart, buy a packet of Casino cigarettes, and return straight home. The store is five minutes' walk from her house. She was seen by a local couple walking down Meadow Avenue, then again by a tow-truck driver in the EZ Mart carpark as he was driving out, and by the clerk. She purchased the cigarettes, left, and was never seen again."

"Fuck. What about statements? Anything helpful from the parents or any of the locals?"

"Not much. Uniforms canvassed the area, there's two

statements that look like they might be worth following up."

"Alright. Go grab the car and meet me out front in ten. We'll go and check out these leads together."

The door to Captain Dodd's office swung open and Police Chief Greaves and Mayor Finn stalked out of the room, storm clouds hanging over their heads. It seemed things hadn't gone well at all. The captain stood at his door and watched them go. He looked sad. Defeated. Dodd glanced over at Brady and motioned for him to come inside.

The captain's office was cramped and filled with piles of files and papers. It stank of cigarettes, bad breath and stale coffee.

"I get the feeling that didn't go too well," Brady smiled grimly, taking a seat.

"You got that right. State Police are officially taking over the investigation Monday morning, but they're working it as of today. There's a task force arriving this afternoon to try and assist in finding the Abby Robbins girl before it's too late. I've been instructed to give them our full co-operation. You're gonna need to be here to help with the transition."

Brady couldn't believe what he was hearing.

"But it's my case. I've been working it for more than a year."

"It's outta my hands, Brady."

"So, what does that mean for us? What, we just hand over all the work we've done to State and let them take all the fucking glory? I'm close on this one Captain, I can feel it."

"Police Chief Greaves says it's all hands on deck till we find the girl. That's Metro and State working together."

"And then what?"

Brady saw the flicker in Dodd's eyes.

"Rankin is going to be re-assigned."

"And me?"

Dodd didn't answer. He didn't need to. The look on his face said it all.

"Fuck," was all Brady could say.

Dodd reached into the bottom drawer of his desk and retrieved a bottle of whiskey and two glasses.

Brady couldn't believe it. They were going to fucking shelve him.

"What, you're gonna put me behind a fucking desk or something?"

"It's outta my hands, Brady."

"Why? 'Cause of the fucking John Bailey case?"

Dodd nodded and filled the glasses. He handed one to Brady, who swallowed the whiskey in one gulp.

"So that's it, is it? Twenty fucking years I've given and for what? They just toss me aside 'cause I made one mistake?"

Dodd shook his head in disbelief. Brady was a good cop; at one point he was one of his best. But in all the time he'd known him, Brady had never taken responsibility for his actions.

It was always someone else's fault.

"Jesus Christ, Brady! You beat that guy half to death. Doctors say he's got brain damage."

Brady looked at Dodd in complete disbelief.

"That fucking piece of shit was drunk... he ran over a fifteen-year-old girl."

"Allegedly," Dodd corrected him. "There's no evidence tying John Bailey to the car that night."

Brady's eyes grew wide with outrage. "He left her dying in the middle of the street. What was I supposed to do?"

"Find the evidence to get him off the streets so he can't do it again."

Brady slumped back in his chair and shook his head like a petulant child. "You know he would have walked."

This pissed Dodd off.

"So instead, you beat him half to death with a goddamned wheel brace. Now he's probably never going to walk again. John Bailey's family is already lawyered up, they're fixing to sue the city and this department."

Brady wasn't having any of it. "This is bullshit."

Dodd looked across at the broken man sitting opposite him. There was no point arguing with him. He could barely see the Brady Hitchcock he used to know anymore. This man was a stranger. Dodd cleared his throat and took a deep breath, regaining his composure, then refilled Brady's glass and handed it to him.

"Look, you're a good cop Brady, but the booze just got the better of you."

Brady's expression changed and he relented, his anger dissipating as the cold hard truth of the captain's words hit home.

He was out of control, and he knew it.

Misery and hopelessness welled in his eyes.

"So, I'm fucked?"

Brady's voice cracked as he spoke, and Dodd couldn't help but feel pity for the man.

"The paperwork hasn't gone through yet. But you'll be on desk duty come Monday morning, pending a formal investigation," Dodd said softly, leaning forward across his desk to make sure Brady heard what he was about to say. "They're talking about criminal charges. If I were you, I'd think about retiring. They ain't gonna let you be a cop again, no matter which way the investigation goes."

Brady finished his drink. There was nothing more to say.

"I appreciate you giving it to me straight, Captain."

Frank Dodd smiled as best he could.

"Anytime, Brady."

Brady pulled himself up out of his chair. He shook the captain's hand before heading for the door.

"Think I'll head out for a bit, maybe follow up a few more leads and do some proper police work while I still got the chance," he laughed, but it sounded empty. "Who knows, maybe I'll find the killer, save the girl and be a hero."

Captain Dodd nodded.

"You do that, Brady. Just do me a favour. Go to that session you got this afternoon with the court-appointed psychiatrist. Stuff like that goes a long way with Internal Affairs."

**9.46 am: Detective Ted Rankin's sedan.**

Brady sat in the front seat of the car in silence, fuming and ignoring Ted Rankin's feeble attempts at small talk, as they weaved their way through the streets towards the first witness's house.

He had walked out of the station in a state of shock, numb and in disbelief, humbled even, by what had happened. He'd been a cop his whole life. What the fuck was he supposed to do now?

If only he hadn't beaten up that guy.

Everything would be different if he just hadn't beaten up that guy.

Same as everything would be different if he hadn't been caught fucking that cocktail waitress... or if he was watching his boy in the bath the night he drowned...

A sickening wave of guilt washed over him as the last few years and the fucking horrible choices he'd made rose up in his throat like bitter, green bile. They replayed over and again in his mind, until he wanted to shout out loud to make them go away.

Brady didn't know all that much, but what he knew, he knew. And one thing he knew was himself.

He wasn't book smart. He could never hold a conversation with an intellectual about philosophy or religion. But he could read people like a book, just by looking in their eyes. He wasn't cultured or educated – in fact he came across as aggressive and obtuse. Yet he had an X-factor about him and could find common ground with almost anyone he met.

But Brady Hitchcock's greatest gift was that he could compartmentalise.

No matter what he did, no matter how he acted, he could pack it up and put it away in a box that he stored in the darkest recesses of his mind, never to be thought of again.

No guilt.

No worries.

No matter how terrible it was.

So, in a moment like this, at a crossroads in his life, instead of experiencing a cathartic moment of self-reflection and accountability, he somehow just moved on and packed it away. Gone in an instant. And as long as he kept moving forward like a shark keeps swimming, and never ever looked in that box in that locked dark room in the back of his mind, he could deal with whatever shit life had to throw at him.

Fuck knows what would happen if all those terrible moments did rear their ugly heads and he had to confront the piece of human garbage he'd become.

By the second bump of coke he did in the station carpark while waiting for Rankin, he'd decided all of this was the captain's fault and not his at all. Brady justified this by telling himself it was the captain's job to stand up for them. To protect them from all the bureaucratic bullshit and not leave them hanging out to dry.

Sure, he said to himself, he'd beaten up that piece-of-shit

perp. But that was nothing new. Everyone did it. And that was the truth. Justice wasn't cut and dried like on TV. The real world didn't work like that. And the truth was if you're on the job, it was up to you to decide how justice was meted out.

That's just how it was.

As a detective, most of the time you had enough to let the courts sort it out. That's because most cases sorted themselves out.

A wife gets killed during a robbery at her house.

The husband did it.

Or her lover.

Or some other fuck that she knows.

Brady didn't know the stats, but if you were investigating a murder, it was almost always someone they knew. It wasn't rocket science, and that was good because the truth is you don't have to be all that smart to be a cop.

But it didn't always go that way. Sometimes, just every now and again, you encountered something entirely different. Some sick fuck who acted with no rhyme or reason any sane person could understand. And that's when you had to make a choice as a cop. A choice between letting some fucking lowlife fucker walk, or making sure they paid for what they'd done.

It was the unspoken rule.

And the captain should have never let it get this far.

Brady sat in the car, lit a cigarette and breathed it in too hard. His mind kept going back to that night and the fucking prick who ran over that little girl.

He should have just kept his mouth shut.

He knew that now.

But he didn't.

His fucking ego wouldn't let him.

He wanted everyone to know, hell, he needed everyone to know that he'd kicked the shit out of that fucking prick John Bailey.

But why?

He muttered to himself and glanced at his partner gripping the steering wheel.

He got his answer. That was why.

It was so he could show those spineless fucking cops like Ted Rankin what real police were all about.

The captain should have praised him for that.

Not this.

He didn't deserve this.

The last two weeks zoomed past his eyes again. If only he'd just kept his mouth shut, none of this would have happened.

It was the story of his life though.

Wasn't long ago that everything was different.

Wasn't long ago that he was a respected cop and a family man with a loving wife and a beautiful daughter. He coached his kid's soccer team on the weekends and volunteered at a "scared-straight" program to help at-risk youth.

But all of that came crashing to a halt the first week of September last year.

Brady, whether he wanted to admit it or not, was exactly like every other "family man" his age approaching mid-life. He was weak. And childish. And although he was a father, he was incapable of taking care of anyone, including himself.

He'd started drinking after his son Neil died. It wasn't anyone's fault. Neil was non-verbal autistic and Brady had simply put him in the bath and gone about doing chores around the house while his wife and daughter were out.

Nobody could have known Neil would have a seizure while he was playing with his toys and drown in a tepid pool no deeper than your ankle.

Brady had always been a drinker. Most cops are. But before Neil passed, it was normally just a beer with lunch or maybe a vodka or two after a hard day. But things changed. Two years after Neil's accident he was a fall-down drunk, wasted at a bar almost every night after work. Shaking down hookers for drugs and a blowjob, or fucking any woman he could find in the back seat of his car before slinking home to his wife and child.

That is, if he went home at all.

Anything to fill the void.

He told himself he behaved the way he did because his wife blamed him for Neil's death.

And maybe that was true.

Brady sure as hell did.

He pitied himself and complained that he didn't feel like part of the family anymore. He even tried to convince himself that his indiscretions were his wife Heidi's fault and not his. But deep down he knew the truth, even if he didn't want to admit it. His wife knew too. She'd always known he was the kind of guy that stuck his dick into anything with a pulse. But at least before Neil died, he'd had the decency to be discreet about it. And as much as she hated him for it, she ignored his philandering because he was a good provider and a good father for their daughter, Ellie.

But nothing lasts forever and, after 11 years of humiliation, Heidi'd had enough.

So, she left him.

Brady came home after working a double shift to find the locks on their house changed and all his clothes packed up in two suitcases that were sitting neatly on the front porch. A note pinned to the top told him she never wanted to see him ever again, and if he came near the house, she'd file a restraining order against him.

This sent Brady over the edge.

Broken-hearted, spiteful and filled with rage and self-loathing, he started drinking all day, every day, levelling himself out with coke and smack and Quaaludes. His work suffered, as did every friendship he had. He blamed everyone but himself for his problems. Instead of looking inward, he lashed out at everyone around until he found himself here... right now...

**10.07 am: 48 Broad Street.**

Brady and Hawkins pulled up out the front of the first witness's house just after 10. His name was Howard Granger and he lived across the road from the EZ Mart.

Brady got out of the car and lit a cigarette, picking a flake of tobacco off his tongue. He surveyed the cold, grey street. A light rain was falling, and wisps of fog clung to the bitumen. Most of the houses in the area looked as though they hadn't been lived in for years; the ones that did were in varying states of disrepair and neglect. It was bleak. Garbage cluttered the street and ugly swatches of graffiti were smeared across almost every wall.

This was a bad neighbourhood.

No money here.

People were so poor here that it seemed they'd just been forgotten and left to fend for themselves.

It was the perfect place for a killer to be hunting.

Howard Granger's house was a putty shade of grey with peeling paint, collapsing gutters and two windows boarded up with plywood. The front yard was filled with rusting junk and long crabgrass.

As he made his way to the front door, Brady noticed with disgust he'd stood in a fresh mound of dogshit. He got rid of what he could with a stick he found in the front yard, then wiped off the rest on the porch.

The door was answered by a hunched-over man dressed in an

old blue robe, dirty grey stubble peppering his cheeks.

"Howard Granger?"

The old man nodded yes and mumbled through his tobacco-stained teeth that people call him Howie.

"I'm Sergeant Brady Hitchcock," Brady said, not bothering to introduce Rankin, who was standing behind him.

"You here about that girl who went missing?" Brady took a long draw on his cigarette and nodded.

"You spoke to some officers earlier this morning, told them you saw something last night. You mind going over that with me?"

The old man nodded and pointed to a filthy brown couch in the room behind him. "I was sitting watching TV, like I always do."

"Remember what you were watching?"

The old man peered at him suspiciously, obviously unimpressed by Brady's inference that he was lying, "It was the late movie."

"Remember what is was?"

"Uh-huh. *Jeremiah Johnson*."

"So what happened then?"

"I heard those kids and their goddammed cars messing around over there in the carpark."

"What kids?"

The old man became enraged at this. "I dunno, those shit birds that hang out over there at the market every night. Local kids. They drive up and down the street racing and ripping up the footpath. I called you a bunch of times about 'em but you never came out."

"So that's what you saw? A bunch of teenagers in their cars?"

The old man frowned and shook his head.

"No. I thought it was them, so I came out to give 'em a piece of my mind. But when I did they weren't there. It was a car. A dark sedan speeding outta the carpark and down Meadow Avenue like a bat outta hell."

The old man pointed down towards the lot.

Trees obstructed the view and Brady noticed most of the streetlights were broken.

"It must have been pretty dark. Are you sure that's what you saw?"

"Dark?" the old man snorted emphatically. "Son, that fucker's lit up so bright it's like it's day most every night."

Brady looked back over at the bright blinking sign outside.

"It's like living next to a goddamned Christmas tree."

"Did you get a look at the driver?"

"Nope."

"How about the make or model?"

"Outside of it being a car, I couldn't say."

Brady nodded in frustration, fished out one of his cards and handed it to the old man.

"Well, if you think of anything give me a call, okay?" The old man nodded.

"Say, you gonna do anything about them kids?"

"I'll look into it."

Brady motioned to Rankin and the two detectives headed for the next witness's house.

**10.41 am: 22 Boulder Lane.**

The uniforms who canvassed had really found fuck all for them to go on. Only two of the witness statements had something of interest to follow up and Brady could tell they were both bullshit just by reading them.

The next witness was Sharon Brown.

She lived two blocks south of the EZ Mart.

Unlike the rest of the neighbourhood, she lived in a well-maintained duplex, decorated in art deco style, with a neatly clipped front lawn and immaculately kept shrubbery along the drive.

Brady knocked on the door and Mrs Brown answered in a huff, her hair in rollers, her make-up half done and a compact clasped in her hand. When Brady asked about what she'd seen, she looked around nervously and lowered her voice, just in case her neighbours could hear her. She said she thought her husband Daryl might have something to do with the girl going missing, and that he had mysteriously gone for a drive last night just before 10 pm.

Brady had seen this shit before.

Chances were Daryl was running around on her. She either knew it and wanted him to pay, or she wasn't quite yet ready to admit it to herself.

Either way, a lead was a lead, and if you had nothing, you followed up everything.

Brady asked what type of car her husband drove.

She said it was a dark sedan and the detectives exchanged knowing glances.

He asked if they could speak to her husband.

Mrs Brown said he was at work till 5.30 pm, but they were free to search the house in the meantime.

The two detectives checked out the premises. Aside from a stack of *Hustler* magazines hidden in the basement, the search revealed nothing. And last time Brady checked, a stash of pornography wasn't enough to pique the interest of a couple of homicide detectives.

When they were done, Brady politely informed Mrs Brown they'd return to talk to her husband when he got home from work.

She seemed less than impressed by this, slamming the door in their faces before Brady had finished speaking.

Brady headed back towards the car. He was already done with this fucking day and it wasn't even 12 o'clock. Just when he thought it couldn't get any worse, Rankin cleared his throat uncomfortably to get his attention and started speaking to him earnestly.

"Look Sarge... ah shit, man, this is hard. Look, I heard about your reassignment, and I just wanted to say how sorry I am."

Brady stopped and bit his lip, barely containing his temper. His hangover felt miserable, his head pounded, and waves of exhaustion crashed over him relentlessly. He needed to do some coke. Or have a drink. Or get a fucking blowjob. He needed anything except for sympathy from this fucking prick.

He would have to ditch Rankin if he was going to make it through the day.

"Save it, Ted. I've been in worse fucking binds than this and come out on top," Brady cleared his throat and lit a cigarette. "Are there any more witnesses from the door knock we should be speaking to?"

"Not that I'm aware of."

"Okay. Well, forensics said to come in around noon; that shouldn't take two of us. You wanna follow up this lady's husband Daryl? Maybe pay him a visit at work?"

Rankin seemed to smile in relief at the suggestion of splitting up. "Sure. I've got a few other leads I could look into."

Brady faked a smile. "Let me know what you find. I'll make my own way back to the station."

Brady watched Rankin jump into his car, gun the engine, and peel off down the street. When he disappeared around the corner, Brady fished out his vial of cocaine from his coat pocket, tapped out a generous bump in the crook of his thumb, and snorted hard.

He absent-mindedly wiped his nose as he looked around the empty street, making sure no one was looking.

Then he headed back to the crime scene.

## 11.32 am: Corner of Broad Street and Meadow Avenue.

Brady stood across the street from the EZ Mart, watching the store and swigging from his silver flask.

It was bitterly cold outside.

He closed his eyes and listened to the rustle of leaves in the wind. He could almost see Abby Robbins walking down the cold, dark street last night in her red sneakers, her nails painted in glitter polish.

He was so close.

He could feel that the Monster had been here. The air had a bitter taste about it, almost as though the killer's presence poisoned everything around it.

Brady crossed the road and stood in the carpark, looking intently at the two tyre marks on the concrete. His eyes followed where they mounted the kerb and sped off down Meadow Avenue.

For no real reason, he followed the tracks down the quiet suburban street.

The trees lining the road ahead were bare and spindly, their knotted branches like gnarled hands silhouetted against the iron-grey sky. The people in their yards or on their porches looked at him suspiciously, obviously still on edge from the events of the previous night.

He passed an unraked yard with a lone child's toy left in the driveway. It was a brightly coloured truck. Dead, brown leaves tumbled around it in the wind.

It looked so sad sitting there, abandoned and forgotten. Melancholy washed over Brady and thoughts of his son sprang into his mind. He never thought about Neil. He didn't let himself; the memory was just too painful. Brady watched as if in a trance as the leaves danced around the little truck. He'd never heard his son laugh while he was alive. Not once. But when he dreamed of him, his little boy would run up to him with arms outstretched, laughing and calling him Daddy.

It was the most beautiful sound Brady had ever heard.

And every time he woke up from that dream, he was crying.

Brady swallowed hard over the lump in his throat and re-trieved his cigarettes from his pocket. He lit one with a shaky hand, drawing on it till made him cough.

It was only then that he realised what he was absentmindedly staring at.

Behind the little toy truck, under a shrub near the fence line of the driveway.

At first, he thought it was just rubbish. But when he stepped closer, he saw an unopened packet of cigarettes.

Casino cigarettes.

The same brand Abby Robbins was sent to buy for her mother.

Brady felt his heart beat faster. The killer must have tossed them out of the car window after he abducted Abby. Brady ditched his cigarette and pulled out a pen from his shirt pocket, grunting loudly as he stooped down and carefully coaxed the packet towards him.

When it was close enough, he fished out a Ziplock evidence bag from his inside jacket pocket and used it to pick up the pack, careful not to touch it with his bare hands. He sealed the bag gently, then held it up in the light, looking closely at the cellophane wrapper.

A smile cracked his weathered face.

There was a print on the plastic wrapper, plain as day. It was a big one too, about the size an adult male's thumb.

Brady checked his watch.

It was coming on to noon.

Time to head over to the lab and see the forensic pathologist, Dr Pyke.

## 12.27 pm: Metro Police Department Crime Lab.

Brady stopped in the hall outside the crime lab, trying to stuff into his mouth what was left of the meatball sandwich he was eating. He made a kind of choking sound as he chewed the mass of bread and meat, then balled up the greasy wrapper and serviette and tossed them into the bin by the door.

It was only then that he noticed a big splash of red sauce on the front of his shirt.

"Fuck," he garbled as he swallowed the last bite, looking around for something to wipe it off with.

There was nothing, so he settled for smearing it off with his finger, then sucking at what was left till it looked clean.

As soon as Brady entered the lab, his nose curled at the acrid smell of cyanoacrylate, iodine, and ninhydrin. The room was small, and it felt cold and lifeless and sterile.

Brady hated coming down here.

The lab itself was well equipped, with sturdy stainless-steel workbenches and counter tops strategically positioned around the room, each organised meticulously with microscopes, scales, arrays of glass beakers, and other specialised scientific equipment. Dr Amanda Pyke was working on the far side of the room at a fume hood. At the sound of the door she glanced over her shoulder, her welcoming smile vanishing as Brady walked in.

"You're late, Sergeant."

"Jesus Amanda, can we be civil? At least try and keep this professional?"

She glared at him, her eyes glazed with venomous rage.

He never should have slept with her.

He did stupid fucking things when he was drunk.

"Professional?" she shook her head in disbelief. "That's rich coming from you, Sergeant Hitchcock."

He deserved that and kept his mouth shut.

The silence between them was ugly. Brady cleared his throat uncomfortably before continuing.

"Anyway, I don't want to take up your time. I found this under a shrub about a block from the EZ Mart."

Brady handed over the evidence bag and Dr Pyke's eyes widened with interest, her disdain for Brady forgotten.

"Do you think this was the packet Abby Robbins was carrying?"

"I hope so."

Dr Pyke made her way over to one of the workbenches, cradling the bag like a newborn baby. She pulled on a fresh pair of latex gloves then unsealed the bag, expertly removing the cigarettes with a pair of long, steel tweezers and placing the packet on a surgical steel tray. She pulled over the arm of a powerful-looking magnifying glass on a stand and flicked on a bright, white light, moving it close to examine the packet carefully.

It took her less than 30 seconds.

"There's traces of blood on the packet here," she glanced back, motioning for Brady to join her. "Let me just dust it quickly for prints. Okay, looks like we've got a partial."

Brady peered closer at the packet as she gently brushed away the black dust.

"Good enough to get a match?"

"Most definitely."

Brady felt his heart beat faster.

This is it, he thought to himself. This is the day I catch this fucker.

"I wouldn't get your hopes up just yet, Sergeant Hitchcock. These prints could be from our perp, or they could be the shop clerk's or Abby's or anyone else who lives on that street."

His smile faded as quickly as it had appeared.

She was right.

"If it's our killer and they're in the system, then we're in business. But I'll need prints from everyone who works in the EZ Mart – and Abby's as well, if you can lift them from her house so we can eliminate them."

"I'll get uniforms on it this right away."

"Good. If I can get this over to the State Police by this after-noon, there could be a hit in a day or two with any luck."

"Can you get it any sooner?"

She glared at him, then relented. She was enough of a professional not to let their bullshit get in the way of doing her job.

Or saving a little girl's life, for that matter.

"I'll do my best, but I'm not promising anything, Sergeant."

"That's good news," Brady smiled. "What else have you got for me?"

"That's where the good news ends, I'm afraid. Abby Robbins was definitely abducted by the Monster. Have a look at this report I'm preparing for the State Police."

Dr Pyke led him over to her desk. There was a series of close-up images of severed fingers next to a typed document.

"See, look here, these bite marks are the same as the Rose and Langton cases. See this denuded bone? He bit her initially with his front incisors. Abby must have pulled away, stripping the finger of its tissue. He's actually bitten her a second time with his molars, causing all this crushing damage and splintering the bone.

"Jesus Christ, can this day get any worse?"

"It can't be worse than Abby Robbins' day," she said simply.

Brady nodded solemnly at this, "I guess we'll find out in the next twelve hours, won't we?"

Amanda cleared her throat and glanced over at Brady. "I heard about what happened with Captain Dodd. For what it's worth, I'm sorry Brady. You're a lot of things, but a bad cop isn't one of them."

"Yeah well, maybe it's for the best," he said. "How'd you find out anyway?"

"Ted Rankin came by a little while ago and told me."

Brady felt bitter contempt rise in his throat. "Fucking little prick," he mumbled.

"Come on, Brady. Detective Rankin's so sweet. Why are you always mean to him?"

Brady snorted at this and shook his head.

"I dunno. There's something about him that rubs me the wrong way."

**1.17 pm: Port Entrance Cafe.**

Brady turned off the ignition of the car he'd signed out from the station. He sat quietly, listening to the engine tick and cool. He was already running late, and he felt like shit, so a couple more minutes wouldn't make a difference. Nothing was going to placate his soon-to-be ex-wife. Brady made sure there was no one else in the carpark, then cut himself a decent line of coke on the dashboard and snorted it. He sat back and let the white-light charge of cocaine arc and branch through his body. He still felt like shit. In fact, he couldn't remember the last time he didn't feel he had an army of ants crawling through his veins. But the coke made everything seem bearable, for a while at least.

Every day was starting to feel the same.

He thumbed a breath mint, locked the car and made his way towards the cafe. The little eatery was in a park at the entrance to Port Perte, with a view of the choppy grey water stretching beyond the breakers to the horizon. It was pretty here. Serene even. Brady breathed in deeply as he made his way across the grass. The air smelt of brine and the wind was cold and bracing.

The park was deserted except for a group of teenagers hanging out near the water's edge. His daughter Ellie was among them, but he pretended not to see her, quickening his pace and popping the collar of his coat.

Brady's wife Heidi was sitting at a table near the back of the café, gazing out the window. She looked up at him with storm clouds in her eyes, frowning as he sat opposite her and motioned to the waitress for a coffee.

"Nice of you to show up," she said. "I've got things to do as well, you know."

"Look, I'm sorry I'm late. I couldn't help it; it's been a shit of a day."

She relented, but her demeanour was icy.

"Did you say hello to Ellie?" Heidi asked as Brady's coffee arrived.

He added two heaped spoonfuls of sugar and shook his head.

"No, I... I didn't know she was here," he lied.

Maybe he could lie to himself and pretend that he didn't know why, but he couldn't face Heidi since she'd kicked him out. Yet deep down in whatever was left of his rotten, bile-filled soul, he knew he just couldn't bare the simple truth: he'd let her down.

He'd let both of them down.

Heidi shook her head in disbelief and disgust. Ellie was sitting with her friends outside the picture window, right beside them. Heidi must have seen him ignore her on his way in.

He tried to change the subject, clearing his throat nervously.

"I'll go say hi in a minute, I promise," Brady tried to smile. But he looked anything but happy; he looked twitchy and strung out like a junkie, "Thanks for meeting me."

"My lawyer said I don't have to speak to you anymore."

Brady nodded and gritted his teeth, trying to keep his cool.

"Yeah, I know. I got his letter."

She could see right through him. She always could.

"So, what do you want?"

"I just want to talk. I mean fuck, how did we get to this? Lawyers? Divorce papers? I don't get it, it's you and me... Babe, look, I know I made some mistakes, but it's almost been a year now, don't you think it's time you let me come back home? You know, give me a second chance?"

She sat back in her chair and laughed ruefully at him.

"A second chance? Brady, you used up all your chances a long time ago. You know, I always knew what you were up to when you were fucking all those other women, but I just lied to myself and pretended I didn't. That was my fault. I don't blame you for that. Just like I don't blame you for what happened to Neil."

That's a lie, he thought to himself. She fucking blamed him for everything.

"After Ellie was born, I thought you'd change, I thought you'd settle down and we could become a real family again. But you're not capable of change or thinking about anyone but yourself. It's always been about you, Brady. What you wanted. You never gave a shit about me and the kids. Then I realised one day that I'd married the wrong man, or at least you weren't the man I married anymore. And I just can't live with that, and neither can Ellie."

"Babe, please. I know I..." Brady started, reaching across the table and trying to hold her hand.

If he could just get her to listen, then things would go back to the way they were, and everything would be alright. But as his hand touched hers, she pulled it away violently and fury blazed in her eyes.

"Don't you dare call me 'Babe' again," she growled, careful to keep her voice low so as not to cause a scene. "I don't love you anymore, Brady. I don't know if I ever did. Can you understand that? I can't live with you ever again. Ellie doesn't need to see you coming home drunk and on drugs, smashing up the house and beating me up, all because you're so high and so guilty and so angry that you can't tell your own life from the horror show that's in your head. I want a divorce, Brady. I want this to be over."

Brady exploded with rage. His temper, which had a hair trigger on a good day, became a blazing inferno, fuelled by cocaine and self-loathing.

"You fucking bitch. I came here today, ready to give you my heart, fighting for our family..."

"Oh fuck you, Brady," Heidi scoffed at him, not intimidated for an instant. She'd endured a lifetime of being scared but was finally in a place where she knew she didn't have to take it anymore. "You're just saying whatever you can right now to try and get what you want. But you don't care about our family; you only want me and Ellie back because you can't have us anymore. You sure as hell didn't give a fuck about the two of us when we were together."

Brady dropped the bravado and protested, his voice becoming high and squeaky.

"That's not true."

"Take a look at yourself Brady. I mean really look at who you've become. What happened to you? Since Neil's been gone…"

"He was my son, he fucking died!"

"He was my son too Brady! Since he's been gone you haven't done a single thing for anyone but yourself. It's all about you. No one else, not me, not Ellie. You asked me to meet you here today to talk about us, but you can't even be sober. It's obvious you're fucked up on drugs…"

He tried to cut in, but she talked over him.

"You need to change Brady, and I hope you can figure that out for yourself, I really do, before it's too late for you. But I'm not waiting around for you to do it. I'm seeking full custody of Ellie in the divorce."

Brady hands clenched into fists.

He wanted to smash her fucking face into hamburger mince.

"The fuck you are," he spat at her through clenched teeth. "Nobody's taking my baby away from me, you hear me? Nobody."

Heidi didn't back down.

"She doesn't want a thing to do with you, Brady. Besides, with your record, when this goes to court my lawyer says the judge will give me whatever I'm asking for."

He smiled at this, seething all the while.

"You'll get nothing. I've got friends on the force."

She smiled at this.

"No, you don't. You're a fucking joke, a dinosaur Brady. No one is gonna stick up for you. You should've done what your friends did, you should've retired years ago. You could've made something of yourself. Maybe we'd still be together, maybe you would've ended up a better person, instead of the piece of shit you are now."

Brady took a deep breath and leaned across the table, staring at her with murder in his eyes. When he spoke, his tone was low and deliberate, his voice loaded with menace.

"I'd rather see you both dead than see you walk away."

Instead of recoiling in fear as he expected, a broad smile of satisfaction spread across Heidi's face from ear to ear. She laughed, opening the handbag bag on the seat beside her and taking out a small tape recorder.

Brady's eyes grew wide, and he shrunk back in his seat.

Heidi held it up for Brady to see, then rewound the tape for a moment before pressing play. His voice was muffled and soft, but it was clearly him talking.

"...see you both dead than see you walk away."

She pressed the stop button with a click and stared at him, letting the finality of the moment sink in.

"You set me up, you fucking bitch."

Heidi shook her head, seemingly tiring of the conversation. "No. You did this to yourself. You're your own worst enemy,

Brady. Sign the divorce papers or this goes to my lawyer, and you'll never see your daughter again."

**2.09 pm: Office of Dr Dawn Wallace PhD.**

The psychiatrist's office was tastefully decorated in wood and chrome, with thick, white shag carpeting and two opposing brown modular armchairs. Brady sat opposite Dr Dawn Wallace, sullen and brooding. Neither spoke; only the sound of a ticking clock filled the silence. After a minute or so, Brady shifted uncomfortably and retrieved his cigarettes from his inside jacket pocket.

"As I said last week, there's no smoking in my office, Sergeant Hitchcock."

He lit one anyway, glaring at her.

After a moment Dr Wallace rose from her chair, retrieved an ornamental crystal dish from a sideboard, and placed it on the table in front of Brady.

"Well, I must say, I'm surprised to see you here today. I didn't think you'd be returning after you stormed out of our last session," she said, sitting down again.

Brady picked a fleck of tobacco from his tongue and flicked it on her pristine white carpet. "Yeah, well it's not like I've got much of a choice."

If Dr Wallace was bothered by this, she didn't show it. Instead, she referred to her notes briefly before continuing.

"I believe last week we were talking about your son, Neil, and the..."

"I told you last time, I don't want to talk about him. Or Ellie either."

Dr Wallace nodded and cleared her throat.

"Alright then Sergeant, let's start with something simple. How has work been this past week?"

"Oh, it's been great, thanks for asking," Brady smiled sarcastically. "I've just been taken off the case I've been working on for over a year. What else, let's see, oh yeah... I'm about to be busted down to desk duty and, to top it all off, I'm facing criminal charges for beating up the prick who ran over a little girl."

"And how does that make you feel?"

Brady looked at her incredulously and laughed.

"Never felt better."

"You know Brady, that sarcasm is really just a thinly veiled attempt to disguise your own feelings of hurt, fear and anger. People often use it as a defence mechanism, a means if you will, of diminishing their own feelings of vulnerability and an unwillingness to acknowledge the deeper underlying feelings."

Brady snorted in frustration and shifted in his chair, looking over at the clock and wishing the hour was done.

"Jesus Christ, what a bunch of fucking psychobabble bullshit. I'm angry, okay, is that what you want to hear? I'm fucking pissed that I took a stand against this piece of shit and every other fucking piss stain like him by making sure the prick didn't get away with it and that fucking justice was served, and no one in the department is backing me up. They fucking hung me out to dry."

Dr Wallace jotted something down in her notepad then looked at him, tapping her lip thoughtfully with her pen.

"You say that you made sure justice was served. Do you think taking the law into your own hands and beating that man was justice?"

Brady nodded. "I'm a fucking police officer. I am the law."

"Surely you don't believe that. I mean, what are the courts for?"

Brady took a long draw on his cigarette and sat forward in his chair, staring at Dr Wallace intently.

"Look, you're not a cop, you don't understand. None of you fucking civilians understand."

"Why don't you try and help me then, Sergeant."

"People like you exist because of people like me. But you're blind to that. You all are. You're so fucking privileged and entitled, and your heads are so far up your own asses that you can't even see what we do for you, what we protect you from. Do you have any idea of the things we see? Do you have any idea what vicious fucking animals people really are?"

"I think that that is a bit of a generalisation, don't you Sergeant Hitchcock?"

"We see society at its worst. We see the murderers and the rapists and the fucking junkies and paedophiles. The sick fucks that murder children and torture fucking animals all 'cause God told them to do it. They're the same degenerate fucks, by the way, that you end up getting out of doing jailtime 'cause you've convinced some fucking bleeding-heart judge that their parents didn't hug them enough when they were children or some other fucking horseshit excuse."

"I'm sensing a lot of hostility coming from you, Sergeant."

"You're damn fucking right I'm hostile. I'm pissed that I have to come here and waste my time, all so you can tell me if I'm capable of doing my job or not."

"Why do you think that is, Sergeant Hitchcock? Do you believe I'm somehow unqualified to determine whether or not you're competent to be in the field, or do you just have some greater issue with psychiatry as a whole?"

"You think you know people, but you don't. You read your fucking books and you listen to your professors and come away with your degree and you think you know people. But you haven't seen what this world can do, the senseless viciousness that exists just beyond the edges of your perfect reality. You come here each day to your fucking office and write your fucking notes and prescribe your fucking pills, but all you do is put people into boxes... predetermined little fucking pigeonholes that you read about in some textbook. See you don't know the first fucking thing about me because you don't know the first fucking thing about life."

"I see."

"You're so blind that you can't even see that the only thing standing between you and complete anarchy is us. The police. We're the thin blue line between civilisation and total chaos. If we didn't do what we do, well, you wouldn't be able to drive to your fucking mansion on the water in your new Mercedes every night after work. You want to know what would happen to you?"

"Alright. Tell me."

"You'd be fucking raped and robbed and murdered before you even got out of the building."

"I see. And do you think I deserve that?"

"No. But I think you've got some fucking nerve to sit there and question how I protect you. You've got no fucking idea what justice is, lady. You know why? Because you've never seen what real injustice is."

Brady stared at her a few moments more before stubbing his cigarette in the ashtray and flopping back in his chair, his point proven. Dr Wallace remained silent for a while. When she spoke again, her voice was calm, even and measured.

"And what is real injustice?"

"How about a cop being persecuted for simply doing his job? How's that?" Brady quipped.

"Is that what you think this is?"

Brady looked at her with contempt and got up from his chair. "This fucking session's over."

He took a step towards the door, then stopped and turned back to her.

"Why don't you try climbing down from your fucking ivory

tower sometime and seeing how the other half live before you dare sit in judgement of real fucking police like me."

Brady snorted in disgust as he walked out the door. "Now if you'll excuse me, I've got some real fucking work to do."

**3.32 pm: Gemini Cocktail Lounge.**

Brady sat at the bar, seething.

He hated that fucking bitch psychiatrist almost more than anyone else he'd ever hated in his life. Truth was, he had started to hate women in general. They were all becoming a huge pain in his ass.

He finished the vodka and lime in front of him and grimaced, then ordered another. He'd have to make his way to the station pretty soon. The captain would be waiting for an update on the case.

Then he remembered.

State Police were taking over.

And he was getting the shaft.

He was drunk enough to chuckle at this. It was probably for the best. He hadn't done anything to help find this girl since he was over at the crime lab hours ago.

His smile faded as he contemplated how he'd failed Abby Robbins. How he'd let his career, his wife, his motherfucking ego distract him from saving that poor little girl.

Maybe it was for the best, he mumbled to himself.

Robbie the bartender fixed him another drink. He slurred thanks, slipped a dollar across the bar, then stood up and made his way to the bathroom.

He was drunk. That was obvious.

Brady needed some coke to level himself out.

The men's room was poorly lit and reeked of the ammonia stink of piss. It was empty except for some degenerate fuck who was lurking around the urinals to sell drugs. Brady considered shaking him down, but he only had to look at him to know anything he was holding would be shit.

Brady went to the urinal instead. He made sure to flash the badge on his belt as he took a piss. By the time Brady had finished, he was alone.

Brady washed up, then dug out a small metal lozenge box from his pants pocket. He flicked open the lid, selected a small, off-white, oval-shaped pill, popped it in his mouth and dry-swallowed it.

He loved fucking Quaaludes.

But that wasn't going to hit for another half an hour. So he retrieved his baggie of coke, cut two long lines on the benchtop near the sink, then snorted one in each nostril with a rolled-up $20 bill.

When he was done, he looked at what was left and swore under his breath.

He was almost out.

There wasn't enough to get him through the night – and he needed more.

Brady glanced at his watch. It was almost four. Shift change at the station was at five. If he could time it right, he might be able to get some from the evidence locker.

But he'd have to get moving.

"One more drink," he said out loud, leaning over the basin
and splashing cold water on his face. The shock of it made
him gasp, and that plus the coke sobered him up almost
immediately.

He looked at himself in the mirror and didn't recognise his
own reflection. Every day felt the same. Nothing was new
or real anymore. He was past the point of pain, everything
was just this numb feeling. In the yellow, sickly light of the
bathroom he looked like a stranger. His face was drawn and
waxy and hollow, as though he was wearing a mask of himself
as an old man.

His heart skipped a beat at the sight.

Then he looked closer and saw the beast he'd become staring
back at him behind his sunken, haunted eyes.

How had everything gone so wrong? Was there a moment
that his life went off the rails, some tipping point that turned
the scales from good into bad? A few years ago, he was on the
fast track to becoming captain.

He had a wife and child who loved him...

The scene in the café with Heidi that afternoon flooded
back to him, drowning him, making him feel like he couldn't
breathe. What did he do? Heidi and Ellie. What the fuck did
he do this afternoon?

He moaned aloud, then it turned into some guttural, an-
guished scream. He grabbed at his hair, trying to tear it

from his head. He stood at the basin for the longest time, spacing out as he stared at the cheap laminate benchtop, his breathing racing like he'd run a marathon, his eyes dazed in a white-out of vodka and cocaine. Then suddenly he snapped alert again, almost as if roused from a deep sleep.

He was disoriented for a moment. Then he came to, his problems forgotten – or at least filed away in some deep, dark recess of his mind where he didn't have to think about them.

The Quaalude was coming on. He could feel it smoothing out the sharp, splintered edges of the coke and the booze, and everything became simple and easy to understand.

He needed more coke.

Brady splashed water on his face and slicked back his hair, then stumbled out of the bathroom. He felt wasted and in control, but when he walked back into the bar everything had changed.

There were five people in the bar at most when he'd gone to the bathroom. It had now come to life. There were people crammed in everywhere. Brady pushed his way through the patrons, back to the vacant stool where he'd been sitting.

He must have been in the bathroom a lot longer than he thought.

The ice in his drink had melted and the condensation on the glass had created a big puddle, soaking through the napkin and spreading across the bar. Brady picked up the drink and swallowed it in a gulp, telling himself one more drink as he slammed the glass back down on the bar ordering another.

That's when the barmaid turned and smiled at him for a moment, then glared at him in fury.

It took several moments for Brady to recognise her.

Then it all came rushing back.

It was the barmaid from this morning that he'd woken up with. The one he'd seduced and had sex with. The one he'd abused and hurled a bottle at as he threw her out of his apartment.

Unbelievably, Brady was so drunk last night, he'd forgotten he'd picked her up from this bar.

"No way. No fucking way." She forgot the other customers in the busy bar and stared at him like he was cancer. "What the fuck are you doing here?"

"Oh... hi," was all he could say.

He'd forgotten her name.

Her eyes narrowed into two slits of hatred. "It's Shelia, you piece of shit. You can't come in here anymore. You're banned."

This was news to Brady. He'd been coming to the Gemini Lounge for 10 years.

"Says who?"

She raised her eyebrows and smiled knowingly, then called out loudly: "Hey Dennis. Can you come out here?"

Brady scoffed at this. He'd known Dennis since he started

coming here and Dennis knew he was police. What the fuck was he gonna do?

"That guy's here. The one I told you attacked me this morning."

"What the fuck are you talking about? I didn't attack you."

It took a few seconds but then Dennis Crawford, the owner of the Gemini Lounge, opened the door marked "PRIVATE" at the end of the bar and lumbered out of the back office. He looked angry, homicidal even. Dennis was imposing and powerfully built, with a boxer's face that looked like it was made of smeared, unfired clay.

In his hand he held a baseball bat.

Before Sheila could say anything, Brady leapt to his own defence.

"Dennis, seriously, I don't even know what this bitch is talking about."

Dennis stopped in his tracks and looked at Sheila in bewilderment.

"That's my brother you're talking to," Sheila Crawford smiled broadly.

Brady felt his hands start shaking and his heart race as adrenalin suddenly coursed through his body, mixing with the coke and the Quaalude.

It felt fucking great.

And as big and scary as Dennis was, Brady knew he'd never hit a cop.

"Get out of here Brady. You ain't welcome in my bar no more."

Brady stood his ground as the crowd of patrons around him seemed to disappear into the darkness.

"Get the fuck out of here? I've been coming to the Gemini for ten years," Brady pushed his glass forward across the bar. "I'll have another. Mine's a vodka and fresh lime."

Brady stared at both of them, then calmly lit a cigarette so they knew he wasn't going anywhere.

The music stopped. Nobody made a sound.

"I'm asking you to leave nice now. I don't want to have to, but I'll put you on your ass if I need to, Brady."

Brady laughed at this. "Are you serious? All 'cause I fucked your barmaid?"

Dennis recoiled from Brady's words like the sting from a punch in the face.

"That's my sister you're disrespecting. You got till the count of ten to get out of here..."

Before Dennis could finish, Brady cut him off.

"What are you gonna do, huh?"

Dennis faltered, his confidence gone, but his sister's eyes flared in anger.

"Shut your fucking mouth you prick," Sheila screamed, swinging wildly at him.

She slapped him hard across the face, her ring catching his lip and splitting it. The entire bar flinched, and Brady's head snapped back hard. He stood frozen and silent for what seemed like forever, and you could hear a pin drop, even over the music. Brady slowly turned back to face Shiela and Dennis, tentatively touching his split lip and examining the blood on his fingers.

He looked at them both and smiled.

He looked simply terrifying.

"So that's it, is it? Is that the best you've got? Huh? Or are you gonna try and hit me with your little bat now, Dennis?"

He spat blood on the bar top and wiped his mouth with the back of his hand.

"I'm a fucking police sergeant," Brady screamed at the top of his lungs. "I could have you both gang-raped in jail a hundred fucking times before someone even came down and took your statement."

Both Dennis and Sheila deflated like balloons.

"You hear me?"

Nobody said a thing.

"Anyone else want to put their fucking hands on me?" Brady looked around the bar, inviting someone to challenge him, but everyone dropped their eyes. "That's what I thought. You fucking pussies."

Dennis let the bat fall to the floor, defeated. Brady grinned, gloating. When neither Dennis nor Sheila said anything more, Brady took a final draw of his cigarette and stubbed it out on the bar, taking his time to burn the countertop.

"You know what? This fucking place sucks."

He picked up his glass and hurled it at the shelves behind the bar, shattering several bottles and the mirror behind. At the loud smash, everyone in the bar jumped abruptly, but no one dared say a thing.

"I don't ever want to see your face in here again, Brady," Dennis mumbled.

"Don't worry, I'm never coming into this shit hole again."

**4.47 pm: Carpark of the Port Perte Metro Police Station.**

Brady sat in the car across from the police station watching the front doors intently, waiting for Detective Roger Crews to waddle his way outside.

Roger Crews was the officer in charge of the evidence locker during the weekday day shift at Port Perte Metro. He had been for the past nine years, taking over from Brady when he was promoted to sergeant.

It wasn't a particularly prestigious job, or a difficult one at that.

Being in charge of the evidence locker basically meant you had one of only two keys to the cage, and you were responsible for keeping a log of who signed your key in and out. Now what happened to the evidence in the locker once the key was signed out had nothing to do with the officer in charge of the key, supposedly because any officer who signed out a key was trustworthy enough to access the evidence locker without supervision. But no matter how much evidence went missing or was tampered with – and it was a lot – if the key was signed for when it was taken out seemed, that good enough for management.

The evidence key was kept in a locked drawer of Detective Roger Crews' desk, third from the male toilets on the far side of the bullpen. And Crews was the only person in the precinct who had a key to that drawer. Well, Crews and Brady, as it had been his desk for five years before that and he'd had the foresight to make a copy before he was promoted.

For a long time, he didn't even really know why he'd copied the key at all. It sat in the back of his drawer in his office at home, unused and forgotten.

But after Neil died, everything changed.

His relationship with Heidi and Ellie changed.

Before Neil died, the four of them were this wonderful insep-
arable unit. A family that loved and supported each moment
in each other's lives. But all that changed. Suddenly Brady
wasn't a part of things anymore and he felt excluded. Heidi
and Ellie seemed to become even closer and, in his mind,
he was left behind. Even though his wife was mourning the
death of her son, and his daughter was only three years old.

He resented them both.

And not for one minute, not ever, did he think it was his fault.

He pitied himself and made excuses. He blamed everyone but
himself.

And he never ever once said it was time to change.

Not long after that he found the key.

Port Perte was a major shipping hub and one of the biggest
sites for drug importation in the region.

Brady checked his watch again.

It was 4.49 pm.

The second shift started at five on the dot. And this was the
great thing about Fridays: Detective Crews and his buddies
always left early on Fridays so they could make it down to
Grady's Bar & Grill before five and get a start on happy hour.
Conversely, Dennis Harrison, the degenerate alcoholic who

was the officer in charge of the evidence locker during the second shift at the station, never showed his face before half past because he was finishing up drinks at Grady's with Crews and his buddies.

Which gave Brady 30 minutes in the evidence locker whenever he needed it.

Like clockwork, Crews and his buddies, detectives Felder and McCarthy, strode through the station door, lingering for a moment as one of them lit a cigarette and the other tied a shoelace. Then they headed north for the two-block walk to the bar.

Brady waited till they'd cleared the carpark before he got out of the car and crossed the busy road. He pushed through the station door and made his way inside. It was busy for this time on a Friday and a noisy crowd was gathered around the desk officer at reception. Brady slipped past without being noticed and made his way into the bullpen.

Inside, most of the desks were already empty and the remaining detectives on shift were either packing up or leaving. No one bothered with Brady – he always worked odd hours and multiple shifts, so him showing up was nothing out of the ordinary. He did notice, however, that Captain Dodd was still in his office and talking to State Police brass and the mayor.

If he was going to do this, it had to be quick.

Brady crossed the bullpen to Crews' desk, opening the drawer and retrieving the key with practiced ease, then pretending to sign the evidence locker log just for show. He walked quickly up the hallway that led to the evidence locker and the records room, glancing around to make sure no one was watching.

There were no surveillance cameras in the precinct.

Brady opened the cage and slipped inside the evidence locker, closing the door quietly behind him. He had to be quick. With the amount of shit he was already in, getting caught in here without authorisation would almost guarantee he was suspended on the spot.

Brady made his way through the maze of steel shelves, each stacked with labelled and sealed brown evidence boxes. He was looking for one in particular: Stephen Jackson, from three months ago. He was caught with four ounces of coke and charged with possession, trafficking, and attempted murder. Brady had helped with the last charge personally, setting up Jackson by hiring some fuck to beat the living shit out of one of his associates and planting physical evidence implicating him.

Narcotics had a field day and seized his entire stash, charging him with attempted murder and making sure he was held without bail.

Stephen Jackson always got the good shit.

Before Brady set him up, Jackson was giving him a taste of everything he brought through the port. Problem was that Jackson became a little too big for his boots and decided he didn't have to give Brady a taste anymore.

Still... there was four ounces of unbelievable coke sitting there, waiting for him.

Brady went through the shelves until he found the evidence box he was looking for. It was sealed with police tape that had been cut and retaped at least five times. Another wouldn't make a difference. Brady pulled the box from the shelf, opening it with a folding knife he kept in his boot. Inside was a stack of files, bagged forensic evidence, and a brick of cocaine so big it would have given Freud a hard-on.

If only he could take it all.

Brady retrieved the almost empty sandwich baggie from his jacket pocket, cut open the brick of coke and shaved off at least a quarter of an ounce. Stashing his score in his jacket, he repackaged the brick as best he could to seem it had never been tampered with.

He put the box back on the shelf and left the evidence room.

The seal was broken on the Stephen Jackson evidence box.

It had been accessed so many times that whoever looked at it next would think it was just a mistake and seal it up themselves. And it didn't matter how much coke was in the box because Jackson was facing charges of attempted murder. Possession was the last thing he or his lawyers cared about.

Brady slipped back into the bullpen and replaced the key.

There were a lot more State Police in there than before.

As he headed back to the carpark, Brady wondered if they had a break in the case. If they had found the Monster he'd been looking for all this time and they were going to save that girl.

Then he thought about that girl.

Abby.

How she was captive to that sick fuck, and he was still officially in charge of finding her safe and alive.

And then Brady thought about how he'd spent the day, maybe her last day, and what he'd tried to do to save her.

And despite how fucked up he was, he cried.

**7.46 pm: Port Perte Metro Police Station.**

Brady walked back into the bullpen, wired and reeking of vodka. It looked different. State Police had set up a couple of desks in the middle of the room and were busy connecting what looked like some kind of high-tech phone surveillance unit. Brady recognised a couple of the state police huddled around the desks; Captain Gibson from this morning's briefing was one of them, along with one of his detectives, William Stone. Most of the other detectives were in the briefing room with Captain Dodd. As soon as Dodd saw Brady walk into the station, he excused himself and stormed out towards him.

"Where the fuck have you been?"

Brady stopped in his tracks, somewhat surprised by his captain's anger.

"What do you mean? I've been working."

"You finished up with the fucking head doctor at three. It's eight o'clock. You were supposed to be here to help brief the State Police for the handover, goddammit. I've been looking for you for hours."

"I'm sorry. Look, I was busy following up some leads."

Dodd looked Brady up and down, noticing his bloodshot eyes, split lip and grey skin. He sniffed at the air and his nostrils flared at the reek of alcohol.

"You smell like a fucking wino," he growled loudly at Brady.

The State Police officers all looked over at the commotion and Captain Dodd lowered his voice to a furious whisper.

"You're the lead detective on this case, Brady..." he started, but Brady cut him off.

"*Was* the lead detective. I'm on a desk come Monday, remember?"

Dodd's eyes widened with fury and his skin flushed a horrible shade of purple.

"Jesus Christ, a little girl's life is on the line and that's all you've got to say?"

Dodd stared at him, his body shaking with rage, until Brady dropped his eyes and shifted uncomfortably.

"You're fucking lucky Detective Rankin was here to cover for you. You be sure to thank him when he gets back from his dinner break."

Dodd gave him one last dirty look and turned to walk away, just as Brady mumbled sarcastically under his breath, "Yeah, I'll get right on that."

Dodd heard Brady's smart-ass quip and glared at him, noticing what looked like white powder crusted around his nose.

"What the fuck is that?" He motioned to Brady's nose and stared at him in disbelief. "Are you fucking high?"

Brady wiped his nose clumsily and sniffed loudly.

"It's allergies, swear to God."

Dodd raised his eyebrows in disbelief.

"Allergies. You're unbelievable, Brady. Alright well, hopefully you're coherent enough to understand what I'm about to tell you. I just got off the phone with the prosecutor. James Bailey handed himself in down at South Port Command, two hours ago."

Brady was confused.

"Who the fuck is James Bailey?"

"He's John Bailey's son. The guy you beat within an inch of his life for that hit- and-run. James Bailey just confessed to stealing his father's car with some of his friends and hitting that poor girl."

Brady couldn't believe what he was hearing.

"You're kidding, right?"

"Do I look like I'm fucking with you?"

Brady started to freak out. This couldn't be right. John Bailey hit that little girl... it couldn't have been his son.

"I didn't know, I mean..."

"They're gonna throw the fucking book at you, Brady. The mayor wants you gone right now; he flat-out said it on the phone ten minutes ago. If you weren't so close with the chief of police, you'd already be suspended from active duty."

"Look Captain, John Bailey did it, I know it. His son's probably covering for him..."

"Why the fuck would his son do that?"

"I don't know..." Brady said, panicking. "So they can sue the city..."

Dodd laughed out loud, shaking his head sadly.

"I'd contact your union rep if I were you, Brady. See about getting a good lawyer. They're talking jail time for this."

Brady felt like he was falling. Criminal charges. He could end up in jail. All because he just tried to...

Just then the police receptionist buzzed in on the phone intercom at the desk in front of him.

"Sergeant Hitchcock, I've got a call for you on line six," she said.

There was something strange about her voice.

"Not now... I'm busy," he snapped at her like she was an annoying gnat.

"Tara, this is Captain Dodd. I really don't think now is a good time..."

Her voice trembled, "It's the killer sir... the Monster. I... think he's on the phone right now. He's asked to speak to Sergeant Hitchcock, sir."

The entire precinct seemed to stop. Everyone looked over in the direction of the phone.

Brady swallowed nervously and reached for the phone receiver. Dodd stopped him.

"Are you sure you're up to this?"

Brady nodded.

Dodd glanced over at Captain Gibson and Detective Stone, who were manning the tracing equipment they'd set up on the precincts line.

"Are we good?"

They gave the thumbs up.

"Remember, you have to keep him on the line for as long as you can," Detective Stone said.

Brady looked at the small, blinking hold light on the phone and thought about the madness waiting for him on the other end. He took a deep breath, picked up the receiver and put line six on speaker.

"This is Hitchcock."

There was no response.

Just silence.

Then a man's breathing. It was heavy and ragged.

"Hello?"

"I've done it again," a voice replied.

It sounded terrifying and deranged, like a nightmare let loose from the deepest pit of hell.

"Done what again?"

No response. Just that heavy, ragged breathing.

"This is Sergeant Brady Hitchcock of the Port Perte Metro Police. Identify yourself."

Heavy, ragged breathing.

Brady licked his lips nervously and glanced up at Officer Stone, who was motioning to keep on asking questions.

"Do you have the girl?"

"Do you know want to know what pain is?"

The voice was like nails on a chalkboard.

"Is Abby Robbins alright?"

"Have you ever touched a knife to the tip of a tongue? Ever watched as the blade slowly slices the meat apart like a slug on a straight razor?"

The Monster laughed and Brady's hair stood on end.

Brady glanced over at Officer Stone again. He made stretching motions with his hand.

"Where is Abby?"

"Do you want to know what pain is? She does... she knows what pain is now..."

"Just tell us where she is. We just want to help her."

The Monster replied with a whisper.

"You can't help her anymore... no one can. She's in the water now."

And with that, the line went dead.

She was dead. There was no saving Abby Robbins.

Brady felt his body go ice cold and he struggled to draw a breath, as though he'd been wrapped in black plastic and dumped in the same watery grave as Abby Robbins.

Brady looked up at Stone, hoping he'd managed to trace the location.

"Did we get him?"

Stone shook his head. Captain Dodd slammed his fist down on the desk in frustration.

"Goddammit!" Dodd shouted, turning to face the large group of police officers gathered in the bullpen. "I want every available officer on the streets in fifteen minutes. Let's see if we can catch this son of a bitch before he dumps the body."

**10.03 pm: Orleigh Park, Port Perte.**

The call came over the police radio at 9.45 pm. Abby Robbins had been found at Orleigh Park, the body washed up on the shore of Port Perte. A couple walking home along the water after a night out at the movies had seen a black plastic bag floating in the water near the seawall. When they dragged it to shore and opened it, they called the police.

Both were now at the hospital, receiving treatment for shock.

No one should ever have to see what they saw.

Brady caught a lift with Captain Dodd, their fight in the bullpen forgotten for the moment. They rode in tense silence, each man steeling himself for the horror that awaited them.

By the time they arrived at Orleigh Park the press was already there, and it was swarming with State Police. Teams of officers were spread out across the grass, scouring the ground for clues, while others searched the shoreline with police hounds that barked and howled loudly in the night. A huge section of the area from the water to the carpark was cordoned off and industrial floodlights illuminated the crime scene. In the middle of it all was a black plastic bag, laid out on the ground and hastily covered with privacy screens.

Brady and Dodd slowly made their way to the body. The killer had taken his time with her. It was much worse than the other victims. Brady looked down at what remained of Abby Robbins. She didn't look real. The lights were so bright and cold they made everything look overblown and lurid, like some kind of sick and twisted horror film.

Brady didn't leave right away. Instead, he stood chain

smoking at the water's edge, watching the dark waves lap against breakwater. He couldn't stop thinking about Abby and her last moments.

He knew she must have been scared, but did she know she was going to die? Was he kind to her? Did he lull her into some false sense of security just so he could pull the carpet out from under her and see the terror in her eyes? Was she locked in some dank fucking basement alone and terrified and waiting for that sick fuck to come in wielding a chainsaw, or was she bound and gagged and blindfolded, blind and afraid and in the dark, just waiting till her horrific ending finally came?

When it did, was it quick and painless? Or did the killer make her suffer?

Did she welcome death's dark embrace, or plead pitifully for her life?

He couldn't help but think of his daughter, Ellie. She wasn't all that much older than Abby. They even probably like the same things... books, music, boys. For all he knew they might have known each other. He'd been a shit of a father to her for as long as he could remember. He didn't want to be. He never wanted to be. Something just went wrong inside him after Neil died. He couldn't connect. He couldn't let anyone close to him anymore, almost as if he was keeping the world at arm's length, just to be sure he would never hurt the people he loved ever again...

Brady took a gulp from his hip flask just as Dodd walked up and stood beside him.

"Anything?" Brady asked.

"No one saw a thing. He could've dropped that bag in the water anywhere."

Brady nodded, taking a final drag on his cigarette.

"Look Brady, about before..." Dodd started, trying to clear the air.

Brady stopped him.

"It's alright Captain. It's been a long time coming. Think I'll head on back home, try and get some sleep."

Brady took a final swig from the flask, then offered him a belt. The captain readily accepted.

"Yeah, you do that Brady. There's nothing any of us can do for her now."

It was true and there was nothing more to be said.

They stood side by side and watched the dark water lap in and out against the breakwater, until Brady turned and walked away.

## 12.15 am: Brady Hitchcock's apartment.

Brady sat on his couch, TV blaring and a vodka bottle in his hand. A baggie of heroin, a burnt spoon and a syringe were among the carnage of crushed beer cans, overflowing ash-trays and discarded takeaway containers littering the coffee table before him.

Every day felt the same.

He couldn't tell them apart anymore.

He couldn't tell what was real and what's a dream, what's a memory and what's a fucking drug-addled hallucination.

He was past the point of pain; everything was numb now.

His life was a movie that he didn't want to watch anymore.

Brady wiped his cheeks and realised he was crying. He took a long, deep swallow from the bottle. Did he drink and take drugs to try to mask the pain, or were the drinking and the drugs the reason he was in pain in the first place?

He didn't know the answer anymore.

Why the fuck was this all happening to him?

Where did everything go so wrong?

The events of the day played over and over again in his head, his mind reliving every excruciating detail until he wanted to scream. He thought about his wife and what he'd said to her... how the fuck could he say those things?

Heidi was going to make sure he never saw her or Ellie again.

Then he thought about Dodd and the department. He lost his fucking job today. What the fuck was he going to do if he wasn't a cop?

He was nothing without that badge...

He was nothing without his girls...

Brady sobbed, his eyes blinded by hot, angry tears that tumbled down his cheeks as he rocked back and forth, moaning to himself.

"They're gonna send me to prison," he slurred.

The cold reality of that fact shone like a searchlight through the fog of his mind.

They were going to send him to prison.

He cried harder, his face twisting like a tantrum-throwing toddler's, all purple and stormy, with a long cord of drool dangling from the corner of his mouth.

Through his tears he could see a news report about Abby Robbins on the TV.

Something about seeing a picture of her smiling face on the screen pulled him out of his funk. In fact, it sobered him the fuck up.

Brady wiped his face with the tail of his shirt and blew his nose loudly on a used napkin. He didn't deserve this. Not any of it. All those fuckers, the ones that were taking him down, they're the ones who deserved this. Brady took a deep breath and reached for the bag and the spoon, measuring out a heavy dose. He half-filled the syringe with water and squirted it over the top, using the back of the stopper to mix the junk. When he was happy, he heated it with his lighter, then dropped in part of a cotton ball and sucked the smack up into the syringe.

He tied his arm off and cleared the air bubbles from the needle, watching a hair's-width stream dart out from the spike.

He didn't deserve this.

Not any of it.

**7.10 am: Brady Hitchcock's apartment.**

The blare of the alarm clock cut through the fog of Brady's hangover like a buzzsaw. He woke with a start, for one endless moment unsure what day it was, who he was, or even where he was sleeping.

Then it came flooding back and he groaned loudly.

As if sensing he was about to roll over and go back to sleep, the alarm clock crackled at him impatiently, the static pure agony in his tender brain.

"Alright, alright. Jesus fucking Christ," he groaned as he cracked open a bloodshot eye and peered blearily over the bedside table. "What time is it?"

The flip cards taunted him: 7.11 am.

With some effort, he reached over and slammed his hand down on the top of the alarm, accidently hitting snooze.

Still, it was quiet, which was good enough for Brady.

He sat up slowly and ignored the ruin of his head. It screamed loudly in protest as he swung his legs out from beneath the covers, planting his feet on the hardwood floor.

It was cold, really cold.

And his bedroom was a disaster.

It looked like the room of some pimply faced shit in a fraternity, not the room of a decorated police sergeant in his forties. The bedside and the floor were littered with empty beer cans, dirty clothes, and a quarter-filled bottle of some cheap rot-gut vodka. A framed family portrait of Brady and his ex-wife with their two kids had the remnants of an 8-ball of coke spilled across the glass.

That was odd.

Familiar somehow.

As Brady tried to stand, his stomach lurched. A wave of sick rolled over him. He felt his complexion sallow as saliva flooded his mouth and cold beads of sweat pearled on his forehead. He sat back on the bed, breathed deep and felt around blindly for the bottle, scared to drop his head too low for fear of throwing up on the floor.

His alcoholic hands were shaking.

When he found the bottle, he expertly twisted off the cap, sending it spinning to the floor like a top. He swallowed deeply. The warm wave crashed over him almost immediately and he swallowed again, then one more time, finishing most of the vodka. Like a cold shadow retreating from the sunlight, he felt the sickness and his shakes start to melt away. The grey light streaming into the room through the tiny window above his dresser started to take on a diffused, golden hue.

It was only then that he noticed there was a woman asleep in the bed beside him.

It took him a moment to process that there was another person in the room.

What was happening?

"Mmm... good morning," she smiled as she stretched sleepily, her eyes hooded and warm and inviting.

Was this déjà vu? Brady blinked and frowned, confused as to what the fuck was happening. Why was everything the same? Why was Shelia Crawford in his bed, just like she was yesterday morning when he woke up?

Did he blank out after he shot up?

It couldn't be.

Shelia and her brother banned him from the Gemini. She fucking hit him in the face last night and split his lip. But here she was, naked, stretching like a cat under the sheets.

Brady jumped out of bed, his heart racing, and he reeled in fear and confusion.

"What the fuck is going?" Brady whispered, his mind reeling.

Sheila ignored his rude tone and stretched seductively across the bed, letting the sheets slip down across her naked body.

"It's so early. Why don't you come back to bed?"

"Why are you here?"

Her smile crumpled into a frown. She sat up, suddenly feeling vulnerable, pulling the sheets over her naked chest.

"What do you mean, why am I here? What's with you Brady?"

He looked at her as though she was pulling some elaborate prank on him.

"Are you fucking with me? Is this some kind of a joke or something? What the fuck are you doing in my house?"

Her feelings of betrayal and exposure gave way to a disappointment she'd experienced too many times before.

"You fucking prick," Shelia snarled, standing up from the bed.

Brady was too confused to notice.

"Yesterday at the Gemini, you told me, your brother told me..." Brady stumbled over his words and stared at her with eyes like saucers, as if he was high on LSD. "You said I was banned from the bar. You said you never wanted to see me again. You fucking hit me in the face!"

She looked at him as if he was crazy.

"No, I didn't. I only met you for the first time last night."

Her words rang like a bell in Brady's skull. He was positive he'd misheard her.

"I just started working at my brother's bar yesterday."

"No, you didn't."

"Baby, I don't know what you were taking last night, but I can assure you that I've never met you before."

The floor fell from beneath Brady's feet.

That can't be true.

"What about what happened here yesterday morning? What

about yesterday afternoon?"

Sheila looked intently at Brady, convinced he was out of his mind.

"What do you mean? I didn't even start my shift till nine. You came into the Gemini about an hour before we closed. You bought me some drinks and we did some blow and..."

She stared at Brady, hoping to prompt some spark of recognition in his eyes.

"You don't remember?"

He shook his head, unsure.

"You tried to have a threesome with me and my cousin. Then you invited me back here and we..."

Brady's eyes narrowed.

"I threw a fucking bottle of vodka at you yesterday morning, then you hit me in the face and gave me this," Brady said, pointing at his bottom lip.

She looked closely. After a moment her expression changed, and she took a tentative step back from him.

The look she gave him said he was the one who was crazy.

"Are you still high, baby?" Her voice was calming, as though she were talking to a child. "Maybe you should go back to bed for a bit."

Brady stopped and stared at her in disbelief.

"Why? What'd you mean?"

"There's nothing fucking there, you weirdo," she replied as she dressed quickly, not even bothering with her underwear.

"What the fuck do you mean there's nothing there? Right fucking here!" he exclaimed as he touched his mouth instinctively, expecting to feel his lip tender and swollen like a balloon.

But it felt normal.

This can't be happening. This can't be real.

She looked genuinely scared of him, like he was a crazy man. On instinct, Brady ran to the bathroom mirror. His reflection looked deranged and hungover, his eyes were wide and panicked, his hair askew. But his lip was completely healed. Almost as though she hadn't hit him at all.

There was nothing there.

What the fuck was going on?

"No, no, no, no, no... This isn't happening," he whispered, as if to convince himself everything was alright.

But his voice was distant. It sounded like someone else was speaking.

"It's the same... you're the same... but everything is different."

He stared at his reflection as his brain tried to process what was happening. There was no fucking explanation. Then he heard her footsteps in the hall and his front door open, so he ran out and stopped her before she could leave.

"Please," he begged.

She stopped and forced a smile. It was obvious she didn't want to be there.

"Look hon, I'm gonna go."

Brady grabbed her wrist.

"Are you fucking with me?" He looked into her eyes earnestly, almost expecting half the precinct to jump out and yell "Surprise!" like this was all some elaborate prank.

Sheila shook her head, smiled and kissed him on the cheek, gently freeing her arm from his grip.

"If I was you I'd drink some coffee or something doll, you know, before you go to work today. I'll see you around, alright?"

Brady stood in his doorway watching Sheila disappear down the stairs. Then, as if on cue, his phone rang.

He walked inside, closed the door behind him and picked up on the third ring.

"Hello?" he said, his voice like a timid child asking, "*Who's there?*" in the dark.

"Brady, is that you?"

Brady nodded, then said, "Yeah."

"Jesus, you sound like shit."

Brady didn't know what to say.

"I'm... I'm okay."

Brady's hands became clammy, and he started to feel faint. This was all too familiar.

"Yeah alright Brady, if you say so. We gotta call, this is serious. Another girl went missing last night."

Brady tried to swallow but the lump in throat hurt.

"The... Monster?"

"Yeah that's right. All Metro officers have been called in to help."

"So... does this mean I'm on active duty again? What about yesterday in your office?"

The line went silent. It was almost 10 seconds before Dodd replied.

"Active duty? Are you fucking drunk or something? You better be ready in fifteen minutes or there'll be hell to pay..."

Brady didn't say anything. The line went dead.

He stood for a moment, trying to understand what was happening.

Did he get so fucked up he hallucinated an entire day?

Was this real, or a dream?

He hung up the phone and looked around the apartment.

Everything looked as it had yesterday. No smack or spoon

on the coffee table. No nothing. He walked to the kitchen and grabbed what was left of a bottle of vodka from the freezer. He closed his eyes and drank till he was almost sick. In his mind the words "*This can't be real, this can't be real*" repeated over and over in his head like a mantra, and he hoped he would open his eyes and see everything the way it should be.

But everything was just the same.

Just like yesterday never happened.

He dressed in a trance, pulling on the first thing he could find on the floor. When he was ready, he cut himself two huge lines of coke, snorted up and headed out the door.

**7.35 am: Detective Ted Rankin's sedan.**

Brady Hitchcock tentatively pushed open the dented double doors of his apartment building and peered outside at the grey, dreary street. Detective Ted Rankin's shitty brown Ford had already pulled up and was waiting at the kerb. Brady hesitated, unsure of what to do. He felt dizzy and sick all at once, as though he'd just got off some horrible fucking ride at the carnival. There had to be a rational explanation for what was happening. Today couldn't be the same as yesterday, it just couldn't. And yet here he was, about to get into his partner's car and head to the same crime scene same as he'd done the day before.

At least he thought it was the same.

Maybe he was still drunk from the night before.

As convenient as that rationalisation was, he simply couldn't believe that was the reason. Brady had basically been hungover on and off for the past 10 years and, no matter how bad it was or how fucked up he'd gotten, there was no way this could be happening as a result.

The junk he shot last night could have been laced with something.

That was possible. Maybe one of those junkie fucks he scored the skag from cut it with PCP or LSD or something. He wouldn't put it past those pieces of shit. If he was tripping it'd explain why he was seeing things. Still, as much as he wanted to believe it, the idea didn't hold water.

There was a third option.

One he didn't want to think about.

Maybe he was losing his mind. Maybe he'd had some kind of fucking psychotic break or something. Maybe the drugs or the pressure from work had snapped something inside his brain and he was completely insane. Out of the three, it made the most sense.

But one thing bothered him.

If you were insane, were you aware of it? Could you recognise that how you were behaving was in fact crazy, but rationalise that you must be sane? Because an insane person wouldn't identify their actions as crazy at all, they'd think they were sane. Could you experience the kind of delusion he was experiencing and be able to rationalise your own sanity and that nothing you were experiencing was indeed as it seemed?

Could you be self-analytical while you were losing your mind?

The loud blare of Rankin's car horn snapped Brady back to reality. He crossed the street and stepped into his partner's car.

"Morning Sergeant," Rankin said as he dropped the car into gear and peeled away from the kerb.

It was if yesterday never happened. As if Brady hadn't lost his job and been humiliated in front of the entire department, including this blow-waved asshole.

Brady nodded hello and remained silent, preferring to retrieve his silver hip flask from his jacket pocket and take a deep swig. Rankin glanced over at him and frowned disapprovingly, but remained tight-lipped, his eyes on the road.

Brady waited for him to say something, anything, reminiscent of their conversation yesterday morning.

But he didn't.

This agitated Brady immensely.

Rankin drove the car in silence towards the EZ Mart crime scene like everything was normal. Like he was expecting Brady to play along and not say something about the fact they were driving to the same crime scene two days in a row. Brady breathed deeply and tried to relax, tried to tell himself there was a rational explanation for what was happening. But he couldn't convince the freak show in his own mind. After a few blocks, he couldn't stand it anymore. If this was a joke, or some kind of elaborate prank, he had to know what the fuck was going on.

"You too, huh?" Brady said.

"What?"

"You heard what I said."

Rankin glanced over at Brady, utterly confused by his sudden, aggressive turn. "Me too what?"

"Are you in on it?"

Rankin gripped the wheel tightly.

"I'm sorry Sergeant, I don't think I know what you're talking about."

"This is all some kind of elaborate joke or something, isn't it?

Did the guys at the station put you up to this?"

"I don't understand, put me up to what?"

"This. The girl this morning, Captain Dodd's call. This whole fucking thing is a prank isn't it?"

"What thing?" Rankin seemed completely lost.

"We just did this yesterday." Brady fumbled for a cigarette and lit it with a shaky hand. His partner's seemingly complete ignorance of what he was saying made his stomach twist in knots.

"Did what? I'm sorry sir, I don't think I follow."

Brady tried to laugh, but it sounded forced and uneasy. "This. The whole fucking day. Come on, you remember, you came and picked me up, we went to the crime scene, then I did a whole fucking report to the State Police."

"I don't know what..."

Brady interrupted angrily. "Yeah, you do. They found the fucking girl in a bag in the river last night. You were there with me; you were right fucking there."

"No I wasn't, Sergeant. We were following up leads on the Kingston homicide yesterday."

Brady fumed and stared at Rankin. That couldn't be right.

That didn't happen last night.

"No, that was Thursday, I'm talking about yesterday. Friday."

Rankin didn't speak right away, and the car fell into silence. It was obvious he didn't want to speak about this with his sergeant anymore.

"Today's Friday, sir. Yesterday we got a call about a boating accident... a girl from the lakes was killed when Jimmy Kingston ran his boat into a bridge. You tried to beat him up in the holding cell..."

Rankin's words seemed to muffle and fade into the ether.

He wasn't lying. He was telling the truth.

Brady felt his mind disassociate from his body. His ears filled with the sound of ringing. Time and light seemed to both compress and then expand around him, causing everything to glow and move at different speeds. Sweat beaded on his forehead and he gripped the seat as if hanging on for dear life. Nausea began to radiate from his stomach, his equilibrium shifting as if he was on a boat in rough seas.

"Pull the fucking car over."

Rankin pulled the car to the side of the road.

Brady fumbled with the door and stumbled out, lurched towards the footpath and started vomiting violently through his nose and mouth. He heaved again and again, as if expelling every fucking toxin from his body, getting rid of the poison of every horrible thing he'd ever said and done, rejecting every moment of this entire fucked-up day until nothing was left but the putrid green bile running down his chin.

When he was done, he wiped the long drip of saliva dangling from his mouth, spat on the grass, and turned to walk back.

Rankin was already out of the car. "Are you okay sergeant?"

Brady shook his head.

"I don't think I know anymore."

## 7.52 am: The EZ Mart.

Brady followed Rankin past the police line and into the car-park. Police buzzed around him, but he barely noticed. It was like he was in a dream, but awake; everything was the same, but nothing seemed real. With every passing moment, Brady felt his grip on reality slip further and further from his grasp.

He was on the edge of screaming and tearing out his hair.

"Sergeant Hitchcock, sir," Officer Dailey said nervously, perturbed by Hitchcock's strange behaviour. "I think, that is, we think it could be the work of the Monster again."

Brady stood mute, staring at them with dull eyes.

Rankin cleared his throat and interjected. "Alright, what have we got?"

"There's a severed finger over there if you want to see it."

They all looked to Brady, who said nothing. Rankin cleared his throat in an effort to get Brady's attention.

"Sergeant? Do you want to have a look?"

After an uncomfortable silence, Brady's eyes came into focus, and he shrugged.

"Uh, yeah, okay."

Brady followed Rankin and Dailey across the lot. Crime scene photographer Steve Gilmore and Dr Amanda Pyke both looked up and said hello, then repeated the exact conversation from yesterday.

Everything played out as it had. The girl's severed finger was curled up on the asphalt in a dried puddle of blood; the lone red sneaker sat on the other side of the lot; there were tyre tracks in the carpark that led in the direction of Meadow Avenue. Through it all, Brady nodded and went along with what was happening, all the while trying his best not to throw up.

Rankin was bent over the severed finger, looking at it carefully.

"Looks just like the others," he said to Dr Pyke.

She agreed, looking at Brady strangely when he didn't say anything. "Injuries look consistent with the other victims. Judging by the lividity I'd say she was attacked about eight to ten hours ago, which fits the timeline."

Just then, Abby Robbins' parents arrived at the crime scene. The girl's mother was hysterical, her face a mess of tears and mascara. Just like yesterday, her husband had to hold his wife to keep her from collapsing on the street as Dailey came running over.

"Sergeant Hitchcock, sir," he said.

Brady didn't answer.

"Sergeant, we just got word from Captain Dodd over the radio. He needs you back at the station ASAP."

Whatever was left of Brady's tenuous grip on reality slipped in that moment. A heavy weight began to bear down on his chest, as if he was having a heart attack.

"I... I... can't do this," he said, backing away, his eyes bugging out of his skull. "I... I can't breathe."

"Sergeant Hitchcock, sir, Captain Dodd told me to tell you that the State Police are coming in for a briefing at nine and if you weren't there you should go find yourself another job."

Anxiety overwhelmed him.

"Are you alright, Brady?" asked Dr Pyke.

Brady shook his head. "I have to go... I can't be here anymore. I need... Detective Rankin, I need to borrow your car."

Rankin hesitated. "Are you sure you're alright to drive sir?"

Brady exploded in fury. "Just give me the keys to your fucking car... NOW!"

Rankin nodded reluctantly and threw him the keys.

"Please be careful, Sir. I'll meet you at the station later."

But Brady didn't hear him – he was already running across the carpark.

**9.25 am: Home of Heidi Hitchcock.**

Brady turned the wheel hard and floored the accelerator as the car roared around the corner into Dowling Avenue. He sped down the quiet suburban street and came to a screeching halt in front of his estranged wife's house.

His old house.

Brady was hyperventilating and in the grips of a panic attack, his heart beating a mile a minute. He kept mumbling, telling himself he was okay, but he wasn't. He was pretty fucking far from okay.

He needed to speak to Heidi. For his whole life, from the day they'd first met, she was his rock. The only person he could open his heart to and talk, the only person who understood him, the only person who could make sense of all the crazy shit in Brady's life.

He needed her now, more than ever.

But he couldn't see her in this state. He was like a frightened, cornered animal.

Brady turned off the engine and tried to get a hold of himself. He could hear birds chirping in the trees and children playing and laughing, so closed his eyes and focused on that, taking deep, slow breaths. The panic faded a little and his breathing calmed. Brady fished out his wallet and popped a couple of Valium he'd been saving for later, washing them down with what was left of the vodka in his flask.

Then he took off his sunglasses and examined his reflection in the rear-view mirror. He didn't recognise the person staring back at him.

It was almost as if he wasn't himself anymore.

When he felt together enough to face Heidi, Brady stumbled up the drive to the house. He knocked on the door and listened for the familiar and comforting sound of her footsteps coming down the hall.

"Who is it?" Heidi asked, opening the door with a smile.

Then she saw Brady and her face hardened.

"What are you doing here?"

"Look, I don't want to bother you, but I don't know where else to go."

She crossed her arms and glared at him.

He tried to smile and break the tension. "I just need to ask you something. I need your help, Heidi."

She sniffed the air suspiciously. "Are you drunk? You're fucking drunk, aren't you?"

Brady was lost for words. This wasn't going how he expected. "I'm not drunk... I..."

Heidi's eyes flashed with anger and she grabbed the door, ready to slam it shut in his face. "You fucking piece of shit. How dare you come to my house drunk?"

"Look baby, it's not like that. I've got a serious..." Brady started to try to explain himself, but Heidi was having none of it. She cut him off angrily.

"Don't you ever call me baby, you fucking shit."

As she moved to close the door, Brady pleaded for her to stop, his eyes filling with tears.

"Please... Look, I don't want to fight. I just want to ask you something."

She stopped, surprised by his sudden vulnerability.

"Do you remember yesterday?" he asked her.

"Are you serious?"

"I couldn't be more serious. Please. Do you remember us meeting at the diner yesterday?"

There was something about him. He looked earnest, defence-less even. "If this is some kind of trick..."

"No, it's not, I promise." Brady ran his fingers through his hair wearily. "Look, can I talk to you Heidi? I'm mean really talk, just me and you like we used to?"

"It's not even ten in the morning and you're falling-down drunk, Brady."

Brady took a deep breath before speaking again.

"I... I... think I'm having a breakdown. Tell me straight okay, did we meet yesterday and talk about the divorce?"

Heidi didn't answer right away. When she did, her voice was

calm and measured, as if at the very end of her patience.

"No, we didn't."

Her reply rocked Brady's mind. He felt as if he was falling, like when an elevator suddenly drops from beneath your feet and your stomach rises up into your throat.

Nothing seemed real.

He had no control.

"I don't know who to talk to about this but you. This all happened, this entire day has already happened... I don't know if it's the drugs or if I'm going crazy, but I'm living the same day again."

Tears tumbled down Brady's cheeks as he looked into his wife's eyes, imploring her to open her heart and understand.

But he was met with contempt.

"You piece of shit. I knew you were fucking high. You think you can fuck with me 'cause you're police? My lawyer said I can get a restraining order against you... he said you'll never see Ellie again!"

"Please, Heidi, please. You gotta help me," Brady begged. "I don't know what else to do. You loved me once, didn't you? Please... I need..."

"I don't give a fuck what you need, Brady. I never loved you... you hear me? Not ever."

All the things they shared, everything they held dear, seemed dead to her. And Brady didn't understand why.

He stared sobbing. He could feel his heart breaking.

"I don't want to see you again, Brady," she said. "I don't want you around Ellie anymore, you hear me?"

Before he could answer, Heidi slammed the door in his face.

**11.05 am: Port Perte Metro Police Station.**

Brady Hitchcock staggered into the station.

He'd finished off another flask of vodka in the carpark and snorted what was left of his cocaine.

Which was a lot.

Normally Brady could handle this and more. But the coke – mixed with the Valium, booze, his broken heart and the last threads of his sanity – fucked him up like a drunk teenager on high school formal night. Everything was a blur; he could barely keep his red-raw eyes focused in front of him. As he showed his face in the bullpen, the door of Captain Dodd's office swung open and the captain stormed out, followed by Police Chief Greaves and Mayor Finn.

"There you are, Sergeant. So nice of you to join us," Mayor Finn said sarcastically.

Brady steadied himself against the desk beside him and nodded, mumbling incoherently.

This pissed off Mayor Finn.

"You were supposed to be here hours ago, briefing us on the Monster case. What the hell have you got to say for yourself?"

They waited.

"I'm sorry sir... I... was..." Brady slurred.

It was obvious he was fall-down drunk.

The mayor regarded Brady with fury. "This is your lead detective, Captain Dodd? A drunk? Look at him, he can barely stand up. No wonder this case is a fucking disaster. I should have your badge, Captain, for allowing this embarrassment to serve on our force."

"Look, this has been a hard morning for all of us. I can assure you that Sergeant Brady is an officer of integrity."

Whatever was left of Brady's rational mind snapped.

He lunged at Finn, grabbing him by his lapels and smashing his fist into his face, breaking his nose in a spurt of snot and blood. Brady threw him to the floor and pinned him, smashing his fist into his face in a crazed fury. Finn's face split open from the force of the blows, his lips, nose and right eye gushing blood.

Dodd and Greaves rushed to restrain Brady. But in his crazed state, he brushed them off and grabbed the mayor's head, slamming it into the linoleum floor again and again and again until it cracked open like a melon. Four more officers rushed in to drag Brady off Mayor Finn. As he was pulled away, Brady started screaming like and animal, screeching about how he was losing his mind, how he was living the same day over again.

**7.10 am: Brady Hitchcock's apartment.**

"What's happening? Are you okay?"

Brady Hitchcock's eyes snapped open, but he wasn't awake. He was still in a dream.

Everything felt like a dream.

"What's happening? Are you okay?"

His booze-soaked, drug-addled mind kicked into gear, and he sat up, looking around, trying to get his bearings.

He was in his bedroom.

That barmaid Sheila was staring at him, her eyes wide and panicked. She looked hysterical.

"Jesus! Are you overdosing?" Sheila scrambled from the bed, pulling the bedclothes across her chest.

Brady looked up at her, trying to say something, anything, but he had no control over his body. His bloodshot eyes rolled back in his head; he curled up into the foetal position and started rocking.

"You're fucking dying?" he heard her ask.

He knew it wasn't a question. It was more like she was trying to explain to herself what was happening. Then he saw her taking in the room: the empty bottles, the coke on the dresser.

Something in her eyes changed.

She pulled on her pants and a shirt from near the bed and found the phone, dialling emergency.

They answered on the second ring.

"Please state the nature of your emergency."

"Shit... uh, yeah, uh, I need an ambulance."

"It's alright, Miss. Take a deep breath."

Sheila glanced over at Brady. It looked like he was having a seizure.

"He's fucking overdosing... please..."

"What is your location?"

He could see her scanning the room, frantically trying to figure out where the fuck she was. Then she grabbed his pants from the floor, and his jacket, tearing at his pockets till she found his wallet.

"Yeah... it's apartment 213, 924 North 25th Street."

Sheila saw his police shield and backed away, dropping the phone and his wallet on the floor. She looked terrified. She picked up the rest of her clothes and ran out of the apartment. leaving the front door wide open.

Brady tried to speak, but nothing came out of his mouth.

It was like he was watching himself, unable to control what he was doing.

The apartment was silent, except for the sound of the emergency operator asking, "Are you there? Miss? Are you there?"

Brady just lay on the bed, unable to move, unwilling to comprehend.

After what felt like an eternity, paramedics crowded into his room and helped him onto a gurney, then wheeled him out to an ambulance. Everyone he knew was there. Captain Dodd. Detective Rankin. All of his friends from the station. They were all smiling, telling him it was okay and he could make it. And when he was pushed into the back of the ambulance and they closed the doors, he could hear them say...

"It's amazing he lasted as long as he did with all the drugs he was taking."

And...

"Hopefully the institution will give him the help he needs."

Brady Hitchcock's life was like a record spinning endlessly on a turntable, the days skipping backwards and forwards between the grooves, the same song replaying over and over again.

He thought these things, and did these things, or maybe he dreamt these things.

He hid from the world and his depression grew. Some days he didn't even get out of bed, and the days he did he drank himself into a stupor. They soon became weeks... Brady rejected reality and time knew no bounds like his own melancholy.

He gazed into the abyss of his own soul and what looked back at him was twisted and angry and full of hate. He had never felt so alone, so betrayed and forgotten. A homicidal desire to extract some semblance of vengeance from the indifference of the universe flared brightly in his heart.

He dreamt horrible things.

Some days he fantasied about getting his gun from its holster and shooting the barmaid while she slept in his bed. Other days, he would lie in wait behind a bush for Ted Rankin to arrive. When he did, Brady would leap out, guns blazing, and blow off his head.

And when he did these things, he felt nothing.

Other days the atrocities were worse.

He killed his ex-wife and his daughter over and over again. He would climb to the top floor of a building with a rifle or burst into a restaurant and open fire, killing indiscriminately until the police ended his rampage with a hail of bullets.

Sometimes it was even worse.

The horror in Brady's mind knew no limits, but all the murders and mass shootings did not break the infernal circle he was trapped within. So, he turned his anger inward, and his self-loathing grew dark and malignant like a tumour. He dreamt constantly of taking his own life until one day, without realising why, he got out of bed and found himself...

**2.34 pm: Office of Dr Dawn Wallace PhD.**

"Are you okay?"

It took Brady a moment to realise where he was.

He'd been living this day for a lifetime.

"It seemed like I lost you there for a minute." Dr Wallace shifted in her chair and chuckled uncomfortably. "Do you do that regularly? Daydream I mean. It seemed like you went somewhere else."

Dr Wallace waited for him to answer. When it was clear he wouldn't, she continued.

"I'd like to address as issue we had last time you were here, when I was asking you about your son."

"I don't want to talk about Neil."

"I know that. But I think we have to address the kind of trauma you must have experienced – and are still experiencing – by losing your son in an accident like that. I believe that one event is the catalyst for every issue you are now facing. I think your willingness to address this painful and pivotal event in your life will mean the difference between you continuing your downward spiral or making effective change."

Brady breathed in deeply to calm his anger.

"I don't want to talk about my son. Not now, not ever."

Dr Wallace shifted in her seat uncomfortably. The tension in the air was unnerving.

"Alright, it's your time Sergeant," she said. "What you get out of these sessions is entirely up to you."

Brady cleared his throat and straightened his jacket.

"Okay. I do have something I want to ask you."

"Go on," said Dr Wallace.

"We can talk about anything, right?"

"Of course."

Everything that had happened flooded his brain at once.

"Well, I don't know how to explain this," he started. "I've been living the same day over and over again."

Dr Wallace didn't react. Instead, she leaned forward with interest, encouraging him to continue.

"It's like I'm trapped in a déjà vu, but it's not one moment, it's an entire day, the same day that keeps repeating again and again. It's been going on for so long... I feel so alone, so trapped. Everything has become meaningless. At first I thought it was all the drugs, or brain cancer. Then I thought I was having some kind of psychosis or a breakdown but now... I... I don't what's real anymore."

"Exactly what drugs are you taking?"

"I drink. A lot."

"How often?"

"Everyday."

"Go on."

"This is confidential, right?"

"Whatever you say in this room stays in this room, Sergeant Hitchcock."

"Okay. Well, I do coke, Quaaludes, smack... whatever gets me through the day."

"And why do you think you do this?"

That was the first time anyone had ever asked that.

It put him on his ass.

"To cope, I guess. You can't see what we see on the job and then come home and play happy families. At least I couldn't anyway."

"And are you coping now? With all the drugs I mean."

"No. I'm so lost right now." Brady sat forward in his seat and gazed at his psychiatrist. He was desperate. This fucking thing had been going on for years. Had it been years? He couldn't tell anymore. "Can you help me? I think I might be losing my mind. Is there something you can do?"

"You said before you felt as if you were living the same day over and over again. Were you speaking literally?"

Brady could see red flags waving in Dr Wallace's eyes.

He chose his next words carefully.

"No... but what's the difference?"

"Well, if I thought you were speaking literally, it would be cause for concern. That type of delusion is very serious and could be a symptom of a much larger problem, like a psychotic episode or DPRD..."

She hadn't mentioned that term before.

"What's DPRD?"

"Depersonalisation Derealisation Disorder. It's a very serious and rare condition. Symptoms can include feelings of alienation and emotional disconnection, as if the subject is living in a movie or a dream, as well as experiencing distortions in the perception of time and not being able to differentiate the past from the present."

"Jesus Christ," Brady gasped.

"But as I said, DPRD is an extremely rare condition. I'd like to pose another possibility. What you seem to be describing to me is some type of existential crisis."

"What does that mean?"

"The human mind has many ways of dealing with stress. An existential crisis is the feeling of unease experienced by an individual when contemplating the very meaning of their existence or the choices and freedoms within it. What is the meaning of life? Am I insignificant in the face of an infinite universe? To put it simply, this anxiety can cause people to feel that their life is inherently pointless. With the breakdown of your marriage and the possibility of not only losing your job but also facing criminal charges and incarceration, it is not all that surprising you feel as if your life is falling apart. If you will, that you have no control anymore," the psychiatrist explained.

"Dr Irvin Yalom identifies what he calls the four ultimate concerns of life: death, freedom, isolation, and meaninglessness. It is not uncommon for somebody confronted with one or more of these concerns to experience problems with addiction and depression, as well as anti-social and compulsive behaviour. When things change dramatically in your work life or in relationships, especially when dealing with feelings of loss, people may relive or even mourn significant moments in their life, regretting decisions they've made and ultimately where that has led them.

"Friedrich Nietzsche once wrote about 'Eternal Recurrence'. He said we are all destined to live the same life over and over again, without change or control of its outcome."

Everything stopped.

Dr Wallace's words hit Brady like a lightning bolt.

It was as if she could see inside his mind.

"Right there, that's what's happening to me." Brady nodded at Dr Wallace enthusiastically and sat forward in his seat. "What you said just then... Eternal recurrence. What is that?"

"Eternal recurrence, or eternal return as it's sometimes referred to, frames existence in terms of endlessly repeating cycles. Put simply, time is a circle, it repeats itself in an infinite loop, and the same events will continue to occur in exactly the same way, over and over again, for eternity. How literally you want to interpret that is up to you. But it would be remiss of me if I didn't point out that this is a philosophical principal, Sergeant Hitchcock, a thought experiment at best, rather than an actual psychological condition," she concluded.

"Can someone actually experience this and be conscious of it?"

This amused Dr Wallace. She sat back and raised her eyebrows with intrigue.

"Eternal return? Well, we are all at the mercy of ever-shifting perspectives, Sergeant. The truth is that, as a cosmological principle, it is not clear to what extent, if at all, even Nietzsche believed in the truth of it. But there was a famous Russian esoteric by the name of PD Ouspensky who did. As a child, he was prone to vivid sensations of déjà vu. When he grew older and encountered the theory of eternal return in the writings of Nietzsche, it occurred to him that this was a possible explanation for his experiences."

Brady remained silent, hanging on her every word.

"He wrote a book about a man who convinces a magician to send him back to his childhood and give him the chance to live his life over again. The magician agrees, but warns him that he will be unable to correct any of his mistakes. This turns out to be true; and although he knows in advance what the outcome of his actions will be, he is unable to keep himself from repeating them. In despair, he asks the magician whether there is any way to change this. The magician says there is, but that he must first change himself – or be doomed to repeat the same mistakes forever."

"How do you mean, change myself?"

"Well, we must all look at ourselves and understand how our actions both create and affect the reality that we live in."

"I think I understand. You're saying that it's the things I do, the way I am, and how I treat the people around me that creates the world I live in. So, in order to change it, in I have to change myself first."

Dr Wallace shifted uncomfortably and cleared her throat.

"Essentially yes, that is true. But I would like to remind you again, Sergeant, that 'eternal return' is a philosophical theory, not a clinical condition. If you are experiencing hallucinations, delusions, or feelings of alienation and emotional disconnection, it could be the symptom of something far more serious and you would require an immediate mental status examination." Dr Wallace looked at him intently.

"Do you understand, Brady?"

He nodded.

She glanced up at the clock on the wall.

"Well, that's the hour. I think we've done some good work here today, Sergeant Hitchcock."

"Yeah, I agree. Suddenly things seem a lot clearer than they did before."

"Alcoholics call that a moment of clarity, Brady. Hang on to it."

He smiled politely and stood up to leave. "Thanks."

She regarded him with concern.

"Do me a favour, would you?"

"What's that?"

"Lay off the bottle and all the rest for a while. Give yourself a break. You might find that the answer you're searching for is right in front of you."

Hours later, he was still pondering her words and how they applied to the shitty life he was living. His mind went back to what his wife had said to him that day at the cafe... how he'd never done a thing for anyone but himself.

She was right.

He hadn't thought about anyone else but himself since Neil had died.

Fuck. Just the mention of his little boy brought a painful lump to his throat. He couldn't let himself think about him, about what had happened the day he died.

Regret washed over him.

No matter what he did, he couldn't change what had happened to his son. Nothing could. He couldn't take back all the pain he'd inflicted on his wife or his daughter, or the hundreds of others he'd fucked over in his life. He didn't want to think about the poor bastard in lying in the ICU. Nothing could change that – he'd fucked up so badly he was probably going to be dismissed from the force, or imprisoned.

You reap what you sow.

There was no changing that.

But he could change what happened next.

He couldn't save himself, but he could try to stop the Monster from hurting another little girl.

## 7.10 am: Brady Hitchcock's apartment.

Brady Hitchcock awoke believing he was still in a dream.

He opened his bloodshot eyes and peered blearily at the blaring alarm clock on his bedside table. Everything was still the same. For a moment he felt himself sink into the heavy black blanket of depression. Then Dr Wallace's words cut through the fog around his alcohol-soaked brain.

Everything would stay the same unless he changed it.

Brady sat up and turned off the alarm, just as the sickly waves of his hangover washed over him. Instead of screaming abuse at Sheila, who was lying in bed next to him, same as she was every day, he shook her gently and smiled as she woke.

Then he asked her to leave.

Sheila flew into a rage and collected her belongings from around the bed in a huff, all the while hurling abuse at him until she slammed the door and left. When she was gone, the apartment was silent and he sat down on the bed and stared at the half-drunk bottle of vodka at his feet.

Our actions both create and affect the reality that we live in.

Brady's hands started to shake and a cold trickle of sweat ran down his back. More beaded on his forehead. The alcohol withdrawal was almost too much for him to handle.

Then the phone rang.

He tried to listen to Captain Dodd's briefing, struggling to swallow the flood of saliva that filled his mouth as the

contents of his stomach lurched and rolled in his oesophagus.
He managed to hang on till the captain hung up, then ran to
the toilet and was violently ill.

His mind may have wanted to change, but his body couldn't
– well not right away anyway. The only way he could get
through the day was to keep on drinking. He was too far gone
to quit cold turkey.

**11.02 am: Port Perte Metro Police Station.**

Brady sat at his desk in the bullpen, reports piled high around him. He'd been reading for hours, looking for anything that might help break the case. The witness statements the uniforms had taken were dead ends. He knew this because he'd interviewed both witnesses. Howard Granger had seen something the night Abby Robbins was taken, but what he saw wasn't going to help them find the Monster.

At best he could corroborate the location of the suspect's vehicle in court.

And Sharon Brown's suspicions about her husband Daryl were founded, but not because he was a murderer. It was because he was a philanderer. Brady could spot that behaviour a mile away.

Takes one to know one.

He regarded the mountain of paperwork before him. It was overwhelming. He was already half asleep and the thought of reading all of this shit made him want to disappear into the bathroom and cut a line. He'd done two when he arrived. He tried his best not to, but it wasn't that easy.

Nothing was easy.

He opened another file. The answer had to be in one of these. A clue, a lead, a piece of evidence someone had overlooked.

Something.

He needed a fucking break.

Brady looked up as two uniforms passed his desk. They looked familiar.

"Hey, did you two do the door-knock interviews for the Abby Robbins case this morning?"

They both stopped and nodded. "Uh-huh."

Talking to Sergeant Brady wasn't something other officers went out of their way to do in Port Perte Station.

"Kember and Horton, right?"

They nodded. He could see how nervous they were. They looked like Laurel and Hardy.

"Got a minute?" Brady asked.

The bigger one, Officer Kember, replied. "Sure Sarge, what can we do for you?

"How'd the interviews go?"

Kember shrugged. "It was late, nobody saw a thing."

Then something occurred to Officer Horton and his eyes filled with panic. "We filed the report, Sir. Didn't Detective Rankin give it to you?"

Brady tried to ease the officer's tension with a smile, but he looked less friendly and more like a shark about to devour them. "He did, I looked through before. You only got two statements. That's pretty light."

Kember started to speak then looked at Horton, confused.

"Three, Sarge."

Brady flicked through the folders on his desk, found the interviews and opened them. "There's only two in the report."

"No sir, we interviewed three people," Kember assured him.

Horton nodded in agreement, pulled his notebook from his breast pocket and skimmed through it till he found the right page.

"Look here. Howard Granger at 48 Broad Street. Umm, Sharon Brown, 22 Boulder Lane, and Doreen Hanson 108 Meadow Ave," Officer Horton said, his finger underlining each name.

Brady sat back in his chair and regarded the two officers. "There's no Doreen Hanson in here. Take a look for your-selves, she's not in there. I can't see a record of the interview at all."

Officer Horton picked up the file. "You mind, sir?"

"Not at all."

They flicked through the report and gave it back to Brady. They both looked uptight. Officer Horton cleared his throat before he spoke. He sounded so formal. "I don't know how that happened, Sir."

"Yeah Sarge, we definitely filed that report," Officer Kember added.

"Well, someone fucked up, didn't they? Enlighten me, who is Doreen Hanson? What did she see?"

Horton scanned his notes.

"Ahh, not too much. She lives alone, in her late eighties, and seemed quite confused. Dementia maybe. She was convinced someone was running through her yard last night."

And there it was.

The answer was in the files. Even if these two were too fucking stupid to put it in there in the first place.

Brady grabbed his coat and headed for the door.

"Where you going, Sarge?" Officer Horton asked.

"Where do you think? To follow up Doreen Hanson."

**12.45 pm: 108 Meadow Avenue.**

The house on Meadow Avenue was two blocks down from the Robbins family's home.

It looked as though it was abandoned. The once well-maintained yard was in disrepair, with overgrown garden beds and fallen leaves left to rot on the ground. Weeds poked up through the ornamental white-pebble drive, and the low-hanging trees at the front of the property cast shadows across the lot. The house stood like a long-forgotten memory, its exterior bearing the weight of time and neglect. Peeling paint exposed the weathered board beneath and the porch sagged under the burden of the years.

Brady got out of the car and looked around. He felt a sense of déjà vu, like he knew this place. There was a house like this on the street where he grew up.

In fact, there was probably house like this in every neighbourhood. It was the odd one on the block that brought down the land values. The poor fucker who lived there was either too senile to look after themselves or too set in their ways to realise they should have sold up years ago and moved somewhere warm.

To the local parents, it was an eyesore. But to the local kids it was revered, a real-life haunted house. A place where you could prove how big your stones were by creeping up to the front door on a dare and ringing the doorbell while your friends hid, watching and giggling nervously behind the front fence. And when the crazy lady who lived there finally answered the door, you'd all wildly bolt in all directions, screaming and laughing in mock fear so the witch didn't get you.

Yeah, Brady knew this place. Growing up everyone knew this place.

He walked up the drive, listening to the soft crunch of white pebbles beneath his feet. A dog started howling out the back. It sounded desperate, as if it was starving or in agony.

There was something about this place, he couldn't shake it. It felt ominous, as if something bad was about to happen. Sure, he was police, but he couldn't shake it. A cold wind rose sharply, and the leaves rustled and whispered as they blew across the yard. Brady walked up the sagging stairs and knocked loudly on the front door.

Nothing.

He knocked again then, after a few moments, put his ear to the door and listened for footsteps. But the house was quiet. He knocked one more time, then walked over to a front window and peeked inside.

It was dark.

Shadows fell across the room, making it almost impossible to see anything in the gloom. Brady wasn't certain but, for a moment, it seemed he could make out the shape of a person on the floor. He tapped on the window and called out loudly to see if it moved, but nothing.

His eyes were playing tricks.

There was no one home.

Brady lingered at the window, then headed back to his car. He got in, turned over the engine, then looked back at the house one last time.

For some reason, goose flesh prickled up his spine.

**8.08 pm: Port Perte Metro Police Station.**

It had been a long day.

After Brady left the house on Meadow Ave, he backtracked to the Robbins home. He stood outside, staring at the building till his feet were numb. Then he walked the route to the crime scene, trying to imagine Abby walking down the same street to the EZ Mart.

It was cold that night so she would have hurried. Most of the streetlights around here were broken, so it would've been dark. She probably wouldn't have known if she was being watched.

But he was waiting for her alright. This didn't happen by chance. The Monster would have parked somewhere along this street and waited for her to emerge, infinitely patient and calculating, like a spider.

But where?

Brady stopped and looked around. The street was lined with maple and oak trees, their branches spindly and bare. It was a full moon the night Abby disappeared. Even with the broken streetlights, she would have been able to see a man waiting in his van if he was parked on the street.

Unless...

Brady walked further down the street towards the corner. There was a thicket of old, sagging spruce down there, the branches hanging low over the street. At night their shadows would be almost impenetrable, no matter how bright the moon was.

142

You could see the EZ Mart from here.

It was the perfect place to lay in wait for her.

Brady walked down to the corner. The gutter was choked with garbage: old cigarette butts, crushed drink cans, clots of leaves and soaked plastic bags. Any of it could have belonged to the Monster.

He crossed the road and stood in the EZ Mart carpark, imagining her coming out of the store, seeing a van with someone enticing her inside. Why did she even go near the van in the first place? Was it money, or did he pretend to be injured? Maybe he just grabbed her and dragged her into the back.

It was impossible to tell.

No one saw or heard a thing.

All that was left were the tyre tracks on the asphalt.

When he had finished at the EZ Mart, Brady headed over to the library where he checked out several books by Nietzsche and Ouspensky that Dr Wallace had discussed with him. He returned to the station and started reviewing the files in the Monster case.

Two murders.

One abduction.

One mysterious phone call.

The two murder victims were Margaret Rose, 14, and Raynor Langton, 12. They lived in different neighbourhoods and went to different schools. Neither victim had anything in common with the other, or Abby Robbins for that matter, except that all three had been picked up by the police for petty crimes. Vandalism, shop lifting, shit like that. Kid's stuff.

There was nothing else linking the three.

It was a fucking dead end. And until he could figure out whether that other phone call was real and if there was another victim out there, he had nothing. Unless he could start reading people's minds, he was...

Then it struck him. It was so obvious. Why didn't he think of it before?

He knew what was going to happen next. The Monster was going to call the station at 8.06 pm and tell him that he'd killed Abby Robbins and dumped her in the water near Orleigh Park.

He knew where he was going to be. And that was two hours from now.

Brady rushed over to the captain's office and knocked. Dodd didn't even look up from his paperwork.

"Make it quick, Brady. I don't have time for your bullshit right now."

"Look, I think I know where the killer is going to dump the body."

Dodd took off his glasses and looked at Brady. "The body? You're saying Abby Robbins is already dead?"

"We need to set up surveillance at Orleigh Park right away."

"How the fuck could you possibly know that?"

"Call it a hunch."

The captain shook his head wearily. He'd heard Brady's bullshit too many times before.

"You're full of shit."

"I'd stake my badge on it," Brady said earnestly.

Dodd laughed at this. "Your badge isn't worth anything, Brady. Besides, the State Police are calling the shots now, it's outta my hands."

Brady bit his lip in frustration. He knew he was right. He had to get to the park tonight.

"Well let me go then. Just let me take a car on my own. Please Captain, you said it yourself, I'm probably facing criminal charges over the John Bailey thing, they'll probably suspend me next week. Let me help, even if it's just for a little while longer."

Dodd harrumphed, then conceded reluctantly.

"Yeah alright. I'll tell Captain Gibson I've got someone covering Orleigh Park. But you go alone, I can't spare anybody else tonight. Some of us police believe we still have a chance of saving that little girl."

"Thanks Captain. I appreciate it."

Brady turned to leave but the captain called him back. "Brady... no more fuck ups. I can't cover for you anymore."

**7.32 pm: Orleigh Park, Port Perte.**

Brady sat alone in his car, parked across from where the body was going to be found in Orleigh Park.

The night air was cool and crisp, and the scent of saltwater was heavy in the air. He felt anxious, nervous even, and his stomach twisted in knots.

The park ahead was dark, bathed only in the soft glow of the streetlights that ran along the pathway at the water's edge. Across the bay he could see the bright lights of the shipyards reflected on the dark water.

The park was all but deserted.

Brady waited and watched in silence.

**9.28 pm: Orleigh Park, Port Perte.**

Brady lit the last cigarette in his pack from the dying embers of the one he'd been smoking. He flicked the butt out the window, silently cursing to himself for not stopping for another pack.

He'd been chain-smoking since he got here.

And the fucking park was dead.

The only movement he'd seen was a family of four walking along the shoreline just after 8.30 pm, stopping to eat dinner at a picnic table near the water. They were there for 22 minutes, then they left.

The Monster would have called the station almost 90 minutes ago.

He had to be close.

The fucker had to be somewhere nearby.

Brady looked around the carpark. It was deserted. Nothing but the sound of distant traffic and the call of nightbirds. For a moment he considered driving back down the boulevard and patrolling the shoreline, but then he saw someone emerge from the shadows by the water up ahead.

He leaned forward in his seat.

It was a couple. They were holding hands and chatting as they made their way slowly along the water's edge.

Could they be a part of it?

Brady grabbed the binoculars from the dashboard and peered at the pair. They were both young, in their twenties. They were talking and laughing the way you did when you were on a date. Then they stopped, and the man pointed at something in the bay.

Brady's heart sank.

He recognised the couple now.

They're the ones who discovered the bag in the water. He swore loudly and slammed his fist into the steering wheel in frustration. The fucker didn't dump the body here. It washed here. And there were more than a hundred waterways feeding into Port Perte. The killer could have dumped the bag anywhere and at any time for the currents to carry it here.

It was going to take a miracle to figure out where the killer dumped the body.

Brady turned over the ignition and revved the engine before tearing out of the carpark, not bothering to wait for the police to arrive.

In the distance he could hear the couple screaming.

**7.33 am: Detective Ted Rankin's sedan.**

Brady got into the car with an angry grunt and slammed the door behind him. He was still fuming about the night before. He'd returned home after the debacle at Port Pert and started drinking, then decided to try reading the books he'd checked out of the library. But the more he read, the angrier and more frustrated he became.

Übermensch.

The death of God.

The Will to Power.

None of it made any sense to him. It was all bullshit. Finally, he threw them out of his window in a fit of rage and smashed up his apartment until the neighbours called the cops and they hauled him off to jail.

He'd woken up in his bed this morning, same as always.

"Good morning, Sergeant," Ted Rankin smiled as he pulled the car out from the curb.

"We need to make a stop."

Rankin cleared his throat nervously.

"Really? Do you think that's a good idea?"

Brady couldn't stand to listen to his fucking voice a moment more.

"We're going to 108 Meadow Avenue before we head to the

crime scene. Don't fucking push me on this, Detective. Not this morning."

Brady glared at Rankin, who looked back at him strangely. "Why do you want to go there?"

"Cause the fucking interview that the uniforms did was missing from the goddamned report."

"What report?"

Brady remembered that the report hadn't been filed yet, as he hadn't arrived at the EZ Mart and sent the uniforms out doorknocking. He backtracked, but Rankin continued to stare at him intently and not watch the road.

"Eyes on the road. I gotta tip, alright?"

"A tip, how the hell can you get a tip? We haven't even been to the crime scene yet."

"Just trust me okay, we won't take long."

Brady lit a smoke and took a long draw.

"I'm sorry, I can't do that Sir," Rankin began. "Captain Dodd was very clear..."

"We'll only be a few minutes, why do you fucking care?" Brady snapped back.

He'd had about all he could take from Ted Rankin today and it wasn't even eight in the fucking morning.

"I've got a job to do, Sergeant. Another girl's gone missing..."

Brady laughed out loud at this. "You honestly think that anything we do matters? I mean really matters? You think that us running around scraping murdered fucking children off the pavement is going to change anything?"

"I do," Rankin replied earnestly.

"All this shit, none of it means anything. This world is a fucking meat grinder. You know that? The same horrible shit is gonna keep on happening whether we're there to clean it up or not. That girl who went missing. She's doomed to spend eternity in some fucking animal's basement, waiting to get torn apart again and again."

Rankin shook his head. "That's not true, Sergeant."

"You don't believe me, huh? Trust me Ted, no matter what you and I do, there's always gonna be another sick fuck out there, no matter how many we put away. We can't save everyone. Truth is, we can't save anyone, no matter how hard we try."

"Jesus Christ can save your soul, Sergeant."

Brady waited for Rankin to tell him the punchline.

"Oh wow, you're being serious. Do you know how stupid you sound right now? This life, it's just the same fucking thing over and over again, all of us cursed to repeat the same mistakes till the day we die. Look at me for example: I have a panoramic view of the circle of shit I'm trapped in, but still, no matter how hard I try, there's not one thing that I can do to unfuck this shitty world around me."

"So, you believe that you have no choice, do you? That all of this is meant to happen?" Rankin asked.

Brady lit a fresh smoke off the butt of his old one. "Again, and again and again."

"I'm sorry Sergeant, but I'm a Christian. I believe we have free will, the choice to do right or wrong. Jesus died for our sins – remember that."

"That's fucking hilarious. No one chooses this. We're dragged into this existence kicking and screaming over and over again, the same messed up bag of meat for eternity. Can't you see it? What, do you think I chose to be who I am? Do you think I want to be a middle-aged cop whose fucking wife and kid won't even speak to him anymore? You think this is something that I wanted to be?"

Rankin looked at him earnestly. "I choose who I am, because I believe that I create my own destiny."

"Then you're a fucking idiot. It's all the same, every fucking day. None of it matters because we can't change a thing about it. No matter what we do, no matter how hard we try we are trapped in the same cycle of abuse, over and over again."

"That's a pretty pessimistic way to look at the world."

Brady almost punched him in the face.

"Oh, fuck you... at least I can see the truth. You've still got your head up your ass."

"You know Sergeant, I feel sorry for you. How can your soul be blessed if it's doomed to return to misery? You know, where I'm from..."

Brady interrupted. "Oh yeah? And what bum fuck town is that?"

"I grew up in Hindley."

"Well let me tell you something. There is nothing, not in your heaven or in this entire fucking universe that's going to deliver me or you or even that poor little girl from this fucking hell here on earth. We're trapped, like rats in a maze for eternity. And there's nothing that can save us. Take me to 108 Meadow Avenue NOW!"

**7.47 am: 108 Meadow Avenue.**

Brady strode up the drive to the front door of the house with Rankin trailing behind reluctantly. He looked nervous about something.

Fucking kiss-ass, Brady thought. He was probably worried about a uniform seeing him here and telling the captain.

Brady knocked on the door loudly and the dog started howling again. This time he could hear movement in the house. The door was answered suddenly by an elderly lady wearing a stained nightdress. She looked like a shut-in; behind her Brady could see a labyrinth of furniture and junk and magazines piled almost to the ceiling.

The smell of mould and rot almost overwhelmed Brady. He swallowed hard and breathed through his mouth to stop himself from gagging.

The old lady eyed him suspiciously. "What do you want?"

"Good morning. Are you Doreen Hansen?"

Her hair was white and thin, sticking up at odd angles as though it had not felt a brush for ages. She seemed confused, angry even, and stared at Brady with a dull, vacant gaze.

"Who's asking?"

"Well ma'am, I'm Sergeant Hitchcock from the Port Perte Police Department."

Her eyes narrowed. "Is this about the dog? I already told that bitch next door it's none of her business."

"This isn't about the dog, I can assure you," Brady said. "I'm here to talk to you about what you saw last night, the people you reported running through your yard?"

"How do you know about that?" she asked, suddenly suspicious.

"You reported it to some of our officers."

Her face slackened and a dull haze of confusion clouded her eyes.

"I did? I don't remember that." She looked over at Rankin, who loitering near the stairs behind Brady. "Who's he?"

"That's Detective Rankin, ma'am. Do you mind telling me what happened here last night?"

Her expression remained blank for several moments before something occurred to her and she came to life again.

"It's those kids. They come round here you know, they come round here and they and mess with my dog. They were down there mucking around in my basement."

"Is there someone in your basement ma'am?"

It was obvious the old woman had taken leave of her senses.

"There was," she said warily.

Brady waited for her to continue. When it was clear she wasn't going to say anything more, he prompted her gently. "Okay, well, did you see anyone last night? Was someone in your yard, or in the basement?"

Mrs Hansen seemed confused by the question and looked over at Rankin again.

"Who's he?"

Brady smiled and tried his best to be patient.

"That's Detective Ted Rankin. Look, is there someone else living here that we could talk to by any chance?"

A smile cracked the old woman's face from ear to ear and she shook her head. "No. No, that's my son. His name is Mark."

Rankin's polite smile disappeared, and he looked at her in complete bewilderment. "I'm sorry ma'am, but I'm not your son. I think you must have me confused with someone else."

Mrs Hansen continued, oblivious to his protests.

"Who's your friend, Mark? Come on in and I'll fix you both something to eat."

Brady glanced back and stifled a snort of laughter. Rankin looked utterly perplexed.

"Ma'am... if you could just focus for a minute. We're here to talk to you about the complaint you made to the police."

She looked at both of them for a moment as if it was the first time she'd seen them.

"Are you the police?"

Brady bit his lip in frustration.

"Yes ma'am. You told one of our officers about someone run-ning through your property last night around ten or eleven o'clock. Do you remember that?"

Her eyes narrowed again lent in a whispered so as not to be heard. "They hate my dog, you know."

"Who? Who hates your dog?"

She glanced over at the house to the right of her property.

"That bitch next door... she hates him. She's always telling me she's going to send the police. They were in my yard last night. That bitch called the police in my yard..."

Mrs Hansen trailed off, then looked at Rankin again. "Who's he?"

Brady smiled as best he could. It was obvious this was just another dead end.

"Alright Mrs Hansen. Thanks so much for your time. We have to go now."

Brady turned to leave, then stopped.

"Ma'am, can I ask you one more question?"

"About what?"

"Do you have any plans today? Is there any reason you won't be home later?"

"I haven't left this house since Mark and I moved in." She smiled at Rankin again. "What's this all about anyway? Who are you?"

The two detectives said goodbye politely, turned and left, making their way down the sagging stairs and across the overgrown front yard towards the white-pebbled drive. The old woman stood at the door, watching them leave. All the while the dog howled miserably from the back yard.

They reached the car and Rankin slid in behind the wheel, turning over the engine and revving it loudly. "Well, that was a complete waste of time. Come on Sergeant, we've gotta go."

Brady looked back at the house again. He didn't know why, but there was something about this place that put him on edge.

"You go," Brady said. "I've got somewhere else I need to be."

**8.35 am: Port Perte Metro Police Station Records Room.**

Brady had managed to slip into the station's records room
unseen by Captain Dodd or the other detectives in the bullpen.
Luckily the State Police, Mayor Finn and Chief Greaves hadn't
arrived for their meeting yet, but it wouldn't be long before
Detective Rankin ratted on him to the captain and the shit hit
the fan.

Good thing was, he didn't think anyone would come looking
for him down here.

He needed a breakthrough.

The Monster was out there and so was Abby, but Brady had
nothing to go on. No witnesses. No physical evidence. Nothing.
But if there was another victim, a third victim just like that
mysterious phone call said there was, then maybe the killer
left something behind that would lead Brady to him.

The records room was deathly quiet, cold, and stank of industrial cleaner. The length and breadth of the space was filled
with floor-to-ceiling shelves stacked with folders and files, lit
from above by harsh fluorescent lights.

Brady started by pulling files on missing children and runaways, from a week before the call until now. For three hours
he combed through papers and files till he found a misfiled
report of a runaway named Joseph King. The boy was reported
missing 12 hours after the third suspected call from the
Monster.

But for some reason he was never even flagged as a possible
victim.

That didn't make any sense to Brady. Why the fuck wasn't this kid flagged? He took a closer look at the case. There wasn't much there in the file and it was obvious Joseph King's disappearance hadn't been properly investigated.

But why?

Two uniforms conducted a preliminary interview with the father, but there was no recorded follow up by a detective. Nothing. Stranger still was that when the case went cold it wasn't passed onto Major Crimes. Joseph King was never even officially listed as a missing person. He'd been filed as a runaway.

None of it made sense. The investigation didn't follow proper procedure. It seemed as if someone had tampered with the file deliberately. As if someone didn't want Joseph King investigated any further.

Brady couldn't understand why. But there was only one way to know, and that was to speak to Joseph King's father in person.

The junk yard was in Cliff Creek, a small township about 40 minutes from town, right on the edge of Port Perte's jurisdiction.

It was pretty. Lots of green trees, blue skies and pristine waterways. You could hear birds and insects instead of traffic, and the air smelled of grass and flowers instead of smog.

This was the kind of place you didn't lock your doors at night.

This was the kind of place you moved to if you wanted to raise a family.

Brady parked his car out front of the junk yard and made his way inside. The property was bordered by a tall wire fence, the lot filled with stacks of old cars, scrap metal, discarded furniture and junk.

Crickets chirped loudly at the midday sun.

Just inside the gate there was a shack with a sign on the door that read:

*"Trespassers will be shot. Survivors will be shot again."*

Brady knocked and waited for someone to answer. After a moment, the boy's father, Jack King, pulled open the door. He greeted him with a big smile plastered across his face. He was short and round with blond receding hair, adult acne and the long-healed scar of a cleft lip.

"Help you with something, mister?" Jack King looked him up and down, sizing him up.

"Yeah hi, I'm Sergeant Brady Hitchcock."

His demeanour soured almost instantly.

"Look, I've had this same conversation with every new cop that starts on this beat. I don't deal in stolen goods. Every one of my transactions is logged and verified..."

Brady shook his head and interrupted.

"I'm not that kind of police. I work homicide. I want to talk about your son, Joseph."

His face crumbled.

All at once Brady's mind flashed back to the horrible day with his son Neil in the bath... No. He couldn't... he could never fucking let his mind go there again. Not now. Not ever.

"Homicide? This about Joe?" Mr King's voice broke as he spoke, his eyes filled with both torment and hope all at once. "You got some news on my boy?"

"Nothing new. I was hoping you could help me."

King's shoulders slumped.

"Yeah of course, whatever you need. I've been trying to get someone back out here for weeks. The last thing they told me was Joe was listed as a runaway."

There it was again. Why the fuck was Joseph King filed as a runaway?

"Yeah, well I'm sorry about that, Mr King."

"You wanna come in, have a cup of coffee or something?"

"Thanks, but we've already wasted enough of your time. I want to talk about the day Joe went missing."

"Yeah alright." He lit a hand-rolled cigarette he had stashed behind his ear and drew deep, exhaling a thick plume of blue-grey smoke before continuing. "It was a Saturday. Joe was supposed to work with me here at the yard, but he wanted to go meet his friends at the boathouse instead, a whole group of them was gonna take their boats out for the day. You know, kids messing about on the creek, that sort of thing. That's nothing out of the ordinary mind you, they did it all the time.

"Anyway, he left about half past nine, a quarter to maybe. Mathias Rousseau, the old man who lives up the way, saw him walking past his place just before ten. He never arrived at the boathouse. I didn't even know till after seven that night. Even then I weren't worried. I just thought he was out late. Wasn't till he hadn't come home past ten I started calling around and checking on him."

"Why that late?" Brady asked.

"Joe's always been a good kid. But he's a wild one. A few months before he disappeared, he got into some trouble with the law. Nothing major, just kid's stuff. He got caught with a bunch of his friends, spray-painting their names on a fence near the school. The police arrested him, but instead of juvie they put him into one of them 'at risk' programs.

"That really changed him, scared him straight. He was different after that. Responsible. He said he never wanted to get in trouble with the police again."

In trouble with the law. Same as the other two victims.

Brady would have to check with in with locals and see what they had on him. There was nothing at Metro.

"I'm sure you've been asked this before, Jack, but did you see anything unusual before Joe disappeared? Any strange customers at the yard, or phone calls? Anything that struck you as out of the ordinary?"

"Nothing at all."

It looked like another dead end.

Fuck.

"All right," Brady said. "Thanks for your time, Jack. Here's my card. Give me a call if you remember anything that might help."

Brady shook Joe King's hand and turned to leave, but before he could take more than a couple of steps King called out to him.

"Well, I'll be, it's you again."

Brady stopped and turned back, somewhat confused.

"Everything okay, Mr King?"

"You're the detective who came out here before, aren't you? You spoke to my wife a few weeks ago."

Brady shook his head. "No, I think you're mistaken. I haven't been out here before. Did a detective come and interview your wife, Mr King?"

"I was away at the time, a detective named Brady Hitchcock came out and spoke to my wife. He didn't leave a card or nothing, but he said he'd be in contact. I called the Cliff Creek station a few times, but I was told Brady Hitchcock wasn't working the case. But it was you, wasn't it?"

"No sir. It wasn't me."

Time stopped.

Everything seemed to change all at once.

King's face became distorted, his eyes a timeless dreamscape colour. All around him reality morphed: the sunlight suddenly seemed to be filtered through some kind of prism, creating a dazzling array that painted the very air. Above, clouds puffed and morphed into a thousand screaming faces, while below, the grass appeared to ripple like a liquid wave, each blade danced and swayed of its own accord. Brady felt the ground beneath his feet become soft and alive, as if it pulsed with the heartbeat of the Earth.

How could this be? He'd never been here before. Well, not that he could remember.

"I'm sorry Jack, when did you say this other detective came out to see you?" Brady was speaking, but he felt he was sitting in the passenger seat in his own head, watching someone else drive.

"As I said, it was a few weeks ago. But I never saw him, I was away at the time. He spoke to my wife." King shook his head. "Sure is strange though, two detectives by the same name, working in the same town that don't even know each other. Never heard of a coincidence like that before."

Brady swallowed hard, his mind reeling.

There was no other Brady Hitchcock.

"Could I speak to your wife at all, Mr King?"

"Well, she's driving up to her sister's place. She should be there sometime tomorrow if you wanna give her a call. This has been awful hard on her."

Great. She may as well be on the fucking moon.

"That's alright, Mr King. I'll be in touch."

**3.37 pm: Mathias Rousseau's house.**

Brady Hitchcock was walking through a déjà vu.

Nothing made sense to him anymore. Not that it had in a very long time. What the fuck was happening to him? Was he living this day over and over again, while re-living other days at the same time without even knowing?

Were there multiple versions of his own self running around, or was someone impersonating him?

The thought of this made him feel sick. It's like lying in bed and trying to comprehend your own mortality, or what you were before you were born, or the endlessness of the universe.

Nothing made sense anymore.

He felt insignificant.

Brady got into the car and tried to calm his nerves, blinking desperately in the hope of ending the psychosis he was experiencing. His breathing was short, rapid and panicked, and he was sweating profusely.

His hands were shaking and he had to press them into his lap to keep them still.

"None of this is real," he said aloud.

But the voice he heard didn't sound convinced.

Brady found a bag of coke in his jacket pocket and attempted to open it, spilling half of it on his pants, the car seat, and the floor.

"Fucking SHIT!" he screamed in utter frustration.

Tears pooled in his eyes and tumbled down his cheeks.

For some reason in this moment, he thought of Neil again. Finding him at the bottom of the tub, his skin blue, his face contorted...

Brady punched the dash as hard as he could, feeling his knuckles crack and split against the faux-wood panel. A white bolt of pain shot through his hand and up his forearm. He cradled it to his chest, sobbing as he had when he'd hurt himself as a child.

It was almost ten minutes before he got a hold of himself.

He examined his hand carefully. Luckily it wasn't broken, just bleeding and bruised and sore. He tore off a strip of his shirt and bandaged it crudely. When he was satisfied, he licked his index finger and carefully pressed it against the coke on his pants and on the seat between his legs, rubbing it on his gums as he went.

The panic and the hallucinations faded.

Brady carefully cut a huge line on the dashboard and snorted it, then washed it down with a deep drink from his flask. He felt better. He sat for a few more minutes, trying to get his breathing under control before he started the engine to drive up the road to see Mathias Rousseau, the last person to see Joseph King alive.

The Rousseau property backed onto Red Cliff Creek. The yard was overgrown and unkempt. The house had seen better days, its exterior weather-beaten: it was once a shade of emerald green, but now most of the peeling paint was criss-crossed with curling fingers of ivy. The grey-shingled roof looked close to caving in and the white-trimmed windows were obscured with decades of cobwebs and dirt.

Mathias Rousseau sat outside near the street on an old lawn chair, drinking a beer and smoking a cheroot, a mottled mongrel dog at his feet. His clothes were old and stained, and he emitted a rather unpleasant odour of fermenting fish. As Brady approached, the dog growled and raised its hackles.

"Rex, get the fuck down," Rousseau snapped at his dog.

When he spoke, he drew out the final syllable of each word, emphasising the last sound.

It was off-putting.

"Mathias? I'm Sergeant Hitchcock from Port Perte Metro Homicide. Mind if I ask you a few questions?"

Mr Rousseau squinted and looked up at him, shading his eyes from the sun.

"What you doing all the way out here?"

"I'm investigating a missing boy."

"Joe King?" Rousseau puffed on his cigar then spat on the ground, revealing a set of rotten brown teeth.

"Yeah. How'd you know that?"

Mr Rousseau smiled and chuckled. It was an ugly sight.

"It's the only thing that's happened round here the past twenty years."

"Well good, I'm sure you'll be able to remember what you saw that day then," Brady smiled politely. "Mind if I ask you a couple of questions?"

Mr Rousseau nodded and sipped on his beer.

"I spoke to Joe's dad Jack earlier. He said you were the last person to see his son. He told me you saw Joe walking past your house here the morning he disappeared."

"Well yeah. But I wasn't the last person to see him."

"How's that?" There was something about this guy that gave Brady the creeps.

"Whoever killed that boy saw him after me. You can be sure of that."

That struck Brady as odd.

"How can you be so sure he's dead?"

Rousseau finished his beer and crushed the can, tossing it on top of a pile on his lawn. He plucked a cold one from the cooler and cracked the ring-pull.

"Last time I checked, fourteen-year-old boys don't just up and vanish into thin air, now do they?"

"Kids run away all the time."

"Not without packing a bag first. That boy walked up the road and disappeared into thin air. He didn't have anything with him but the shirt on his back. You see many runaways like that?"

Brady shook his head, surprised at Rousseau's eye for detail.

"No sir I don't. Do you remember the day Joe King went missing?"

"Uh-huh. I was sitting right here when he come by. It was five to ten in the morning."

Brady raised his eyebrows at this.

"How do you know that? I mean, that's a pretty specific thing to remember."

"It was my birthday. My son came and picked me up for lunch not five minutes after."

"Did your son see him too?" Brady asked.

"No sir. As I said, he arrived five minutes after."

"I don't suppose you saw anything else unusual that day?"

Rousseau puffed on his cigar thoughtfully. "No. After lunch I spent the afternoon at my boy's place up in Ramhead Bay. He drove me back here around seven. Well, now there was something come to think of it." Brady felt his heart beating faster.

"And what was that?" he pressed.

"Well, when I got home, Rex here was making a hell of a fuss about something round the back of the house. I remember 'cause I thought someone had broken in. But when we checked we couldn't find anything."

"That's it?"

Rousseau nodded and sipped his beer.

"Alright. Mind if I take a look around?"

"Be my guest."

Brady walked around the house. It was a big property backing onto Red Cliff Creek. The yard had been left to run wild, knee-high grass stretching off to the tree line near the water. Near the back of the house were two ramshackle buildings, a tool shed and an outhouse. Nearby was an old washer and dryer that had been left out in the elements to rust.

He pushed open the door to the old outhouse. It creaked slowly as it swung open and the stench of decades of waste rushed out to great him. He coughed and buried his mouth and nose in the crook of his elbow as he pulled the string for the light. The bare bulb sputtered and glowed a dim and sickly yellow light. There was nothing in here but a couple of crumpled skin mags and a pyramid of toilet paper against the back wall. Bloated flies flew in circles around toilet hole, alighting occasionally on the shit-splattered seat to feast. He peered into the pit latrine below and gagged, cursing to himself for not bringing a flashlight.

He couldn't see anything down there.

It was the perfect place to hide a body. The stench alone would cover the smell of a decomposing body perfectly and no one in their right mind would want to go down in there and shift through a river of shit to find a corpse.

He smiled at the thought of Ted Rankin having to go down there and look for Joe King. In fact, for a moment, he actually considered calling it in.

The tool shed looked like it hadn't been used in years. The door had rusted shut and inside there was nothing but old tools, cobwebs and the smell of old motor oil.

Brady picked his way down through the long grass to the creek. Gnarled and twisted trees grew along the banks and in the murky water, their branches heavy with Spanish moss. Stepping into the shadows of the tress was like passing through an emerald curtain. Beyond, the air was heavy and stagnant, the sun shone through the gloom in thin, bright beams and insects buzzed around Brady's face. There was a derelict, home-made jetty jutting out into the water ahead, nothing more than algae-encrusted rotting wood with an aluminium boat tied to the end. Brady carefully walked to the end of the crumbling pier and looked out to the water, his mind a mess of cluttered confusion.

He felt numb, everything was distorted.

He could feel himself losing touch with what was real and what wasn't. He felt almost as if he was watching himself, watching his own thoughts.

Was there two of him?

The water beyond was blanketed in shadows. It looked more like a marsh, the stream clogged with the moss-covered trunks of fallen trees and thick vegetation. Without even thinking, he untied the boat and stepped aboard, pushing himself away from the jetty and out into the darkness.

**4.16 pm: Red Cliff Creek.**

The light had started to change, and twilight was fast approaching.

The boat slipped silently through the murky water while golden rays of sunlight pushed their way through the thick canopy of trees above. Frogs and toads croaked from hidden corners and the water murmured softly as it ebbed and flowed with the tide.

Brady could hear his own heartbeat in his ears.

Nothing seemed real.

He could not tell the past from the present anymore.

The world was becoming a dream.

The boat drifted through the brackish water. It was littered with garbage. A half-submerged body of an old, rusted car peeked up from the depths. Discarded tyres and old plastic bags cluttered the exposed tree roots.

"What am I doing out here?" Brady said out loud.

He gazed out across the scum-clogged water. There was nothing out here. This was another dead end; this whole day was another dead end. The Monster was a dream, some fucking recurring nightmare that slipped in and out of reality... much like Brady himself. Were they destined to play this horrific game of cat-and-mouse for eternity?

Maybe they were linked somehow.

Maybe Brady was the Monster all along, and he was searching for himself.

Something caught Brady's attention up ahead, snapping him out of his psychotic spiral. There was a mass of tangled refuse snagged on a slime- covered log, a black garbage bag with what looked like a long, white branch poking out of the top.

He guided the boat through the muddy water and a foul waft of decay drifted out into the air. He felt his heart skip a beat then start to pound in his chest. As the boat drew closer to the log, the sickly-sweet odour intensified, like some malevolent spirit guiding him towards the horrors of the secret it kept.

The buzzing of insects filled the air, and Brady gave an involuntary shudder.

As the boat floated closer, he could see through the eerie gloom ahead. The white branch poking out of the top garbage bag was not a piece of wood.

It was a bone.

The femur bone of a human.

Brady paddled closer and the bow bounced gently off the log. He reached out and grabbed the algae-covered wood with his hand to steady the boat. Flies and gnats swarmed, and the air was filled with the unsettling and overwhelming symphony of decay. He swatted the bugs from his face and grabbed hold of the slick bag, carefully freeing it from its mooring.

As Brady hauled the bag up over the hull, it split open across the deck boards. The malodorous stench of decomposition exploded like a stink bomb. A slime- coated, putrefied skeleton spilled out, still partially clothed in a black Led Zeppelin T-shirt and blue jeans, the same outfit Joe King was said to be wearing the day he disappeared.

It was horrifying and exhilarating all at once.

The smell was overwhelming. Brady did all he could not to vomit as he leaned in to examine the corpse. Almost immediately, he noticed saw marks on the bones beneath the boy's head, and more on his arms and legs. His right index finger was missing, the bone jagged and broken as if it had been bitten off.

Just like the other victims of the Monster.

It had never been found.

He gingerly patted the boy's jeans for the bulge of a wallet, finding one in the back pocket. There was a library card inside that read "Joseph King". He tried the front pockets. A set of keys in one, and a handful of white pebbles in the other.

There was no doubt now that Joseph King was the third victim of the Monster.

**9.35 am: Port Perte Metro Police Station Records Room.**

Brady pulled an old cardboard archive box from the top shelf and grunted with the effort as he laid it on the cold, linoleum floor. He sat down beside it, flipped the lid, grabbed the top file and started skimming through it. When he was done, he dropped it on the floor and read the next one. He'd been doing this ever since he dragged that poor kid's body out of the swamp. There were more victims of the Monster out there. More kids, lost or long forgotten, crying out to be found from some watery grave.

He was sure of it now.

But that wasn't all.

All three victims had criminal records. Nothing major, but they'd all been in trouble with the law. That was the only thing they had in common. Other than that, they appeared to be totally random. None of them lived near each other, they all went to different schools, two of them came from working-class families, the second victim's family was well-to-do. From what Brady could piece together from the limited evidence he had, there was not another thing linking these kids, except for the fact they'd each been found torn apart, dumped in garbage bags in waterways around Port Perte.

So maybe that was something.

That got Brady thinking about the Joe King's case. How it wasn't investigated properly, how he was somehow listed as a runaway instead of a missing person, and how his file had been tucked away like someone had tried to hide it.

Was there a cop involved in this? Or someone impersonating one?

Was that why Jack King's wife thought she'd spoken to Brady about her missing son?

The files were a dead end. He couldn't remember how long he spent poring over case after case, but at some point he sat back and realised that he could spend months or even years going through the shit stored in the records room and the basement without even getting close to finding anything.

There had to be another way.

He went to the desk, picked up the phone and started calling other jurisdictions, asking if they had any cases involving victims matching the Monster's MO. He was met with a wall of silence. Most of the detectives he spoke to were either too busy to share anything, or simply just didn't give a fuck to take the time to look.

The ones that did want to help had nothing fitting the Monster's profile.

Until he called Shawcross PD.

"Bill Morgan." He sounded uptight and busy.

"Yeah hi Bill, it's Brady Hitchcock from Port Perte Homicide."

"Oh, hi Brady, what can I do for you?"

"Bit of an odd question, you got a minute?" Brady asked, hoping to hell he wouldn't get shut down again.

"Shoot."

"I've gotta couple of cold cases I'm looking into here, three teenagers, two female one male. All of them had records. The killer's MO is consistent... all the victims were abducted from public places, in each case the killer bit off the right index finger. They were all found dismembered in black plastic garbage bags and dumped in waterways. We have no finger-prints, no hair or fibre evidence, and no witnesses. You got anything like that?"

"Jesus," Morgan sighed. "Uh, geez. Nothing comes to mind."

"Cold case maybe?"

"I don't think so," Morgan paused to think. "Well, nothing unsolved anyway."

"What do you mean?" Brady asked.

"We had a something like that here a few years back, a run-away found wrapped in plastic and dumped in a water tower... but from what I can remember, the case was prosecuted."

"You remember her name at all?" Brady asked.

"Hang on a sec," Morgan said. Brady could hear his hand cover the receiver and his muffled voice calling across the bullpen. "Hey Pamela... do you remember that case from a few years back with the girl in the water tower?"

The line went silent, and Brady's stomach began to churn.

Morgan came back on the line. "Girl's name was Rachel Dunston. I can get the file copied and overnighted to you if you want."

Brady's whole body shivered. It had to be the Monster.

"Look, I'm kinda in a rush. Is there any chance I could speak to one of the detectives who worked the case?"

"I think Gus Croft was the lead on that. He's transferred out of Homicide now though."

"Is he there? Can I have a word?"

"Well, here's the thing. Old Gus has been off the last few days. Out of town. You see, his sister died."

This wasn't good.

"Is there any way I can get a hold of him?"

Morgan hesitated before he answered. "I think he was staying with his son..."

"You got a number?" Brady asked anxiously. He could feel this lead slipping away.

"I do, but he'd already be on the road. He's coming back today so there's really no way to reach him," Morgan explained.

"Fuck," Brady growled through gritted teeth as he strained to contain his frustration.

"He's due back at the station tonight though. Gus and his partner are working night shift on account of the fair being in town this week."

"Really?" Brady sat up in his chair. "What time?"

"Shift starts at eight."

Brady checked his watch.

It was 12.30 pm. Shawcross was nine hours' drive from Port Perte.

"Tell Gus that I'll be there before ten. You tell him to wait for me, alright?"

"Sure, I'll tell him," Morgan said, but Brady had already slammed down the phone and grabbed his jacket.

This could be the break he'd been looking for.

**9.17 pm: Shawcross Police Station.**

Brady raced straight through from Port Perte without a stop.

He was dog tired, drunk and high. But more than anything he was desperate that this would finally be the break that led him to the Monster.

He checked in and was escorted to the bullpen. Detective Gus Croft was waiting for him at his desk. He was in his early sixties with slicked-back thinning hair and a droopy moustache flecked with the remnants of his dinner. His nose and cheeks were ruddy and swollen and bumpy.

He greeted Brady with a wide smile and a handshake.

"How was the drive?"

"Long," Brady said as he took a seat next to Croft's desk. "Thanks for seeing me."

"You must be beat. My partner's getting herself some coffee, you wanna cup?"

Brady could smell the waft of whiskey coming from Gus Croft's cup and agreed readily. "Yeah sure, that'd be great."

The old detective turned in his chair and waved in the direction of the kitchenette on the far side of the bullpen, trying to get the attention of a 30-something detective who was busy pouring herself a coffee from the percolator.

When it was obvious that she could see Croft, he resorted to yelling across the room.

"Kate?"

She turned at the sound of her name and looked over with an annoyed expression.

"You mind grabbing our guest from Port Perte here a cup while you're up?"

She nodded yes, begrudgingly.

Brady couldn't help but notice how tall she was. She was well over six feet, with white-blonde hair and blue eyes.

Croft slid a file across his desk to Brady.

"Well, here's the Rachel Dunston file. Sergeant Morgan had a copy made for you before he left for the night. You know you didn't have to drive all this way. I could have mailed it and saved you the time."

"I appreciate that, Gus. But I needed it today. You mind giving me the broad strokes?"

Brady opened the file and started leafing through it while Croft spoke. The photos of the victim were eerily similar.

"Rachel Dunston was reported missing by her mother two years ago. She was a troubled girl, sixteen years old, came from a bad home. Both the mother and stepfather were alcoholics and in and out of jail. She had a pretty long record herself, two stints in juvie, one for drugs, one for grand theft auto. The initial investigation listed her as a missing person but the feeling 'round the station was she'd picked up and run off. It wasn't until the manager of the building she used to live in got complaints about a strange taste in the water that her body was found."

Croft's partner, Detective Kate Hazelwood, arrived with the coffees and introduced herself.

"You want some?" Croft asked as he fished a bottle of rotgut whiskey from the bottom drawer of his desk, pouring a measure into his half-drunk coffee.

Brady nodded yes, though Detective Hazelwood declined.

"Go on, you were saying." Brady sipped his coffee. It was hot and strong and good.

"Well, the apartment building Rachel Dunston lived in had an old water tower on the roof. A few of the residents had started complaining to the super that their water tasted funny and had a bad smell. As you can see by the pictures, she was found stowed away at the bottom of the tank."

Brady flipped through the photos. They were horrifying. The atrocities committed on her poor little body were beyond imagination.

Brady tapped on one picture of her hand. "I see her right index finger is missing. Did you recover the digit, or receive any anonymous calls about the abduction?"

"Nah. If the finger was left somewhere we didn't find it. Then again, no one was looking for it either. She was missing for about three months before she was found. Could be a pet or vermin ran off with it, I dunno."

"Any calls to the station claiming credit for the homicide?" Hazelwood interjected. "There're no records of any calls to the station or the family. Gus and his former partner who worked this were pretty meticulous."

Brady looked up from the file.

"So all of this was before your time?"

She nodded. "Yeah. I transferred in eighteen months ago from over in Hindley."

It took Brady a moment to remember where he'd heard the towns name before. Then he realised Rankin had mentioned it to him.

"You don't say. My partner's from Hindley too. Maybe you know him, Detective Ted Rankin?"

"Can't say that I do."

"You sure? Tall guy, mid-thirties, tremendous pain in the ass? He transferred to Port Perte about the same time you came to Shawcross."

She shook her head, blowing on her coffee before taking a sip.

"I worked in Hindley for ten years. I never met anyone by that name."

A strange feeling came over Brady. He could feel the threads of his own thoughts slipping through his hands. He struggled to hold himself together.

"My partner took this case pretty personally. Rachel Dunston was one of the kids at the at-risk program he ran for troubled teens."

Brady felt the world around him go numb.

A high-pitched noise sounded in his ears. The "at-risk" program. Joseph King was a part of an "at-risk" program for troubled teens. The Monster's first two victims, Margaret Rose and Raynor Langton, both had police records.

Croft kept talking, oblivious to the stunned look on Brady's face. "Anyway, we ended up arresting the stepfather for it. He always denied it, but he had no alibi and a history of domestic violence, so it wasn't hard to get a conviction. He got life, but only served two years. Hung himself in his cell. Hope that helps you. Got any more questions?"

Brady was shaking. He felt as if he was in a vacuum.

He swallowed hard and spoke slowly and carefully, afraid his head was going to split open and his brain spill out on the desk.

"What was your old partner's name again?"

"Mark Mason. Why?" Gus replied, finishing the rest of his coffee and pouring himself another shot of whiskey.

Brady's voice was shaking. "Have you got a photo of Mark at all?"

"Sure, I've got one around here somewhere."

Croft took another sip from his coffee and fumbled around in his desk, retrieving a small, wooden-framed black-and-white photo.

It was of Gus Croft and Ted Rankin.

The floor suddenly fell out from beneath Brady's feet.

Ted Rankin was Mark Mason.

Ted Rankin was the Monster.

Brady felt the sick rise up in him.

"Excuse me a sec. I gotta go to the bathroom."

Brady raced across the room and burst into the bathroom, kicking open the first stall door and vomiting into the toilet bowl. He threw up again and again, his body in spasms as vomit poured out of his nose and his mouth. It was as if somehow he was purging all of the horrors of the case from his being. After what seemed like an eternity, the nausea subsided and he started to cough and dry heave. Spent, Brady fell to the cold bathroom floor and started to cry so hard his whole body convulsed.

How could he have been so stupid?

It was right there in front of his face – and he never saw it.

The fucking Monster was beside him every step of the way.

**1.32 am: Brady Hitchcock's car.**

Brady gripped the wheel tightly as his car sped south down the highway towards Port Perte.

It was raining hard, and Brady struggled to keep the car in its lane.

He was so tired.

Not just tired and sleepy, but exhausted. Exhausted by this case and his job, the fact that his wife and daughter hated him, and the ever-present, soul- destroying fucking guilt of his son's death which bore down upon his heart with such a crushing force it made it almost impossible to breath anymore.

But most of all, he was exhausted by life.

He didn't want it anymore.

This life was a curse and nothing more.

Brady blinked the tears from his eyes. The highway before him was a mess of bright strobing lights, their elongated trails streaking across his field of vision. Back in the Shawcross PD bathroom it had taken him almost 20 minutes to pull himself together. When he had finally stopped crying and regained control of himself, he cleaned up and popped two Quaaludes to calm his nerves.

He spent the next couple of hours trying to find out as much as he could about Detective Mark Mason. After a couple more drinks, Croft let him into the records room and Brady was able to access Mason's personnel file.

He was a decorated officer, a favourite of the brass who ran an "at risk" youth program and had an almost perfect arrest record. Apparently, he'd retired early to care for his elderly mother. That had come as a surprise to the department as he'd been earmarked for promotion. There were no records of where he'd moved to after he left the force.

When Brady dug a little deeper, he found some sealed records from Mason's childhood. He was orphaned at a young age, his parents killed in an horrific murder suicide, his mother shooting his father then herself over an alleged affair. Mason had witnessed the killings and was found sitting with the bodies, completely catatonic. After a year in hospital, he was made a ward of the state and sent to the infamous Christian reformatory school Governor's House, which was eventually closed after multiple allegations of physical and sexual abuse by the priests. He was adopted when he was 10 years old, although the name of the family wasn't mentioned in the records.

In his file there was a picture of Mason as a boy, standing with his class in front of the school's entrance. Carved above the door were three monkeys.

One covering its eyes. One covering its ears and one covering its mouth.

See no evil. Hear no evil. Speak no evil.

Just like the Monster said on the phone.

In every case, the Monster's victims had their eyes, ears and tongues removed and then their eyelids, ear canals and mouths sewn shut. He was almost sick again when he thought about their horrible torture. It was almost midnight by the time he left.

Brady sped down the highway.

Hours passed.

Everything was a blur. The highway stretched ahead of him, the sound of his screaming drowning out its hum. Nothing seemed real. It was as if he was sitting behind himself, watching like a passenger as he drove the car.

Ever obsessed about a moment in time and wished you could do it over again and make it different?

Brady gripped the steering wheel tightly and shook his head to clear it.

## 7.10 am: Brady Hitchcock's apartment.

Brady Hitchcock woke as if still in a dream. He opened his bloodshot eyes and, after a moment, the events of last night came flooding back to him. He sat bolt upright in bed, turned off his alarm and gently woke the woman sleeping in bed beside him.

"Shelia? Shelia, you've got to wake up."

Sheila Crawford moaned sleepily and opened her eyes a crack.

"Mmm... good morning." She rolled over and smiled at him with warm, dusty eyes. "What time is it?"

"It's early," he answered softly. "I'm sorry to do this but something's come up, and I have to go into work."

She stretched seductively across the bed, letting the sheets slip down across her naked body.

"Do you have to? Why don't you come back to bed?"

"I wish I could, really I do. But we've just had a major break in the murder case I'm investigating and I have to go."

Shelia nodded and got out of bed, grabbing her clothes and dressing.

He could see she was disappointed.

"It's okay, I understand. You got coffee?"

Brady shook his head, looking around the disaster of his

bedroom. "Haven't done the shopping in a while I'm afraid. In fact, I haven't done a lot of things round here in a while."

She laughed at this.

"I can see that. Look, I'm working at the bar tonight, but I don't start till nine, why don't we get some dinner if you're not busy."

"Sounds great. But I don't know how long I'm going to be tied up today. Can we take a raincheck? How about I call you later and let you know if I can make it."

She kissed him on the lips and headed for the door.

"Call me, okay?"

The phone rang as she left.

"Hello?"

It was Captain Dodd.

"Brady, is that you?"

"Yeah Captain."

"Jesus, you sound like shit."

Brady couldn't help but smile.

"I'm alright."

"We gotta call, this is serious. Another girl went missing last night, looks like our killer's back again."

"The Monster? I'll be ready in fifteen."

"I'll send Detective Rankin by to pick you up."

The phone buzzed dead in his hand. Just the sound of Ted Rankin's name made Brady's skin crawl. He had to be careful. He had to play this right. There was no point arresting Rankin until he found out where he was hiding the girl. He had to save Abby Robbins. That meant Brady needed to make sure the Monster didn't suspect he knew a thing.

### 7.32 am: Detective Ted Rankin's sedan.

Brady Hitchcock lit a cigarette and glanced over at Ted Rankin from the corner of his eye. The tension in the car was so thick you could cut it with a knife.

"You mind opening your window, Sarge?" Rankin coughed uncomfortably.

He had to figure out a way of tricking him and somehow get an idea of where he might have stashed the girl. Brady rolled down the window and tossed out the cigarette.

"That better?"

He could see Rankin was surprised by this.

"Sure."

"Where'd you say you grew up again?" Brady asked, as offhandedly as he could.

Rankin looked at him strangely.

"What's that, Sarge?"

"Hindley right? That's where you grew up, isn't it?"

"Yeah, that's right," Rankin nodded, and a smile cracked his face. "Born and raised."

He must make him believe he was interested.

"You were on the force there, weren't you? Before you came here, I mean."

"Uh-huh. Six years on the beat. Then two more in Narcotics before I transferred to Homicide."

He was lying. That was how long he served up in Shawcross – Brady read it last night.

"You still got family there?" Brady asked casually.

"They died years ago."

"Oh, sorry to hear that. So, what prompted the move here?"

Rankin shrugged. "Hindley is a sleepy little town. Nothing much ever happened there. I wanted a chance to work in a place where I could do some good."

"So where are you living now?"

That was too much. Rankin glanced over at him suspiciously.

"I've got an apartment over in a new development on Port Perte. Why all the questions, Sarge?"

Brady needed to back off.

"No reason. Just making conversation."

Rankin raised his eyebrows and nodded.

"Oh. Alright," he said. He seemed sceptical all of a sudden.

It took every fibre of Brady Hitchcock's being to not grab Ted Rankin by the throat and beat him till he gave up where he was hiding the girl.

He had her somewhere right now.

The fucking prick.

But he couldn't risk it. Not yet. Not till there was no other option. There had to be some other way of figuring this out.

## 7.46 am: The EZ Mart.

Brady made his way through the throng of onlookers and past the police tape, calling Officer Dailey over to talk.

"Can you bring me up to speed?" Brady asked as he surveyed the crime scene, hoping something might jump out at him.

Dailey went through the same routine he always did, and Brady listened and nodded, all the while keeping Rankin in his peripheral vision. When Dailey was finished, Brady walked over to where Steve Gilmore and Dr Amanda Pyke were examining the finger. Then the girl's parents arrived as if on cue, her mother screaming hysterically, and then Dailey interrupted them telling Brady he needed to head back to the station for a meeting with Captain Dodd and the State Police.

"I'll go take care of the parents, Boss. You go see the captain and I'll meet you at the station later."

Brady stopped him. He couldn't let Rankin out of his sight, not for a fucking second, or he may never find Abby Robbins alive.

"You know what, the captain can wait. Detective Rankin, you finish up here with Dr Pyke. I'll go bag the shoe and speak with the parents, then we'll drive to the station together when I'm done."

Rankin shrugged and nodded, squatting down next to Dr Pyke to talk about the finger.

Brady grabbed an evidence bag from Dailey and crossed the carpark quickly, hoping to bag the girl's shoe before the parents noticed it.

He thought of Neil again, dead in the bottom of the bath. Brady hadn't heard a thing...

No. He couldn't think about that now.

Not now.

He reached the shoe and bent down to pick it up, then stopped dead. There was something near the shoe. Something he'd never seen before... something that wasn't in any of the reports or in any of the evidence from the crime scene. A tiny, decorative white pebble was lying on the bitumen right next to the shoe.

Why hadn't he ever noticed this before?

It was the same as the pebbles he had found in Joseph King's pocket when he fished him out of Red Cliff Creek.

"Oh shit," he whispered to himself.

Brady looked back at Rankin crouched next to Dr Pyke. Caught in the tread of his sneakers were small, white pebbles... the same kind of pebbles that adorned the driveway at 108 Meadow Drive, where that little old lady lived.

The house just down the road from where Abby Robbins lived.

It all made sense. Doreen Hansen, the woman with dementia they had interviewed, had called Ted Rankin "Mark". She thought he was her son. That's because he was her son. She must have adopted him when he was a boy. Rankin must be hiding the children he abducts at her house. And the poor woman is so confused she wouldn't have a clue what was going on.

She wouldn't know there was murderer in her house.

Half the time she wouldn't probably even recognise her own son. That's why she thinks there are kids messing around in her basement. It's been the Monster the whole time, probably torturing and dismembering these screaming children while she watched the fucking *Price is Right*.

But why hadn't he seen this before?

Then it hit him. Every morning at the crime scene, Brady had always sent Rankin to console the parents, so he didn't have to deal with them. The fucking prick must have noticed the pebble and hidden it when he was bagging the shoe. The answer was right there in front of him the whole time, just waiting to be found.

But Brady had been too blind to see it.

He bagged the shoe and the pebble, handed them to a uniform, then crossed the carpark and spoke with the girl's parents.

"Mr and Mrs Robbins, I'm Sergeant Brady Hitchcock," he said. "I want to assure you that I'm going to find your daughter alive."

As Brady spoke, he glanced back over his shoulder at Rankin. But he wasn't talking to Dr Pyke or the uniforms anymore. He was standing by himself, watching Brady.

It was unnerving.

Their eyes met. And the Monster was staring back at Brady with cold, dead eyes.

**10.32 am: Port Perte Metro Police Station.**

The drive back to the station was tense.

Neither Brady nor Rankin spoke to each other.

Brady could feel he suspected something, but what he couldn't tell. Did he know that Brady knew? Had he seen him pick up the pebble? Was it all the questions in the car?

Something had tipped him, but Brady didn't know what.

When they arrived at the station Brady attended the State Police briefing then followed Captain Dodd into his office for their meeting. All the time he was there he watched Rankin in the bullpen.

When Brady was done being fired, he walked out into the bullpen and Rankin came over to speak to him.

"Look Sarge... I heard about your reassignment, we all did, and I just wanted to say how sorry I am."

Rankin looked at him strangely as he spoke, his eyes were flat and devoid of feeling. It was as if he had no emotions at all inside.

"Don't worry about it. It's been a long time coming. Anyway, I've got a few things to take care of before the meeting with forensics at noon. You mind doing these follow-up door knock interviews without me this morning?"

Rankin smiled as if relieved, but it didn't touch his eyes.

"No problem. I've got a couple of other things I can look into as well."

Brady smiled and nodded. "Great, take your time. Just let me know what you find, okay?"

Rankin grabbed his coat and car keys. "Yeah sure. I'll be back in this afternoon."

Brady watched him leave.

As soon as Rankin was out of sight, Brady ran down to the motor pool and signed out one of the department cars. By the time he reached the carpark he could see Rankin's shitty brown Ford driving down the street in traffic.

Brady followed, careful to keep at least a block between them.

Rankin's Ford drove south towards Meadow Avenue and the EZ Mart crime scene, just as Brady thought he would. He knew he had Abby stashed at the old woman's house. All the evidence pointed to it. But Brady wasn't going to make a move until he saw Rankin pull up in front of that house and walk inside.

Although Brady was pretty positive that Abby was at that house on Meadow Avenue, he wasn't certain, and there was too much at stake.

He wasn't going to take a chance with Abby Robbins' life.

Not till he was sure.

The car tracked south, then after 10 blocks turned east towards the Port. This put Brady on edge. Why the fuck was he heading towards the port? He has said he had an apartment there. Was that where Abby was being held? Or was this his routine, something he did to make sure he wasn't followed?

If Brady were a killer that's what he'd do.

In fact, he'd take a different route every time.

Brady followed, careful to stay back. The shitty brown Ford started driving erratically, weaving through traffic. Then he made a sudden turn, flying down a side street for a few blocks before heading back onto the main road.

Brady sped up and tried to stay with him, all the while doing his best not to alert Rankin that he was being tailed.

The traffic became heavier.

As if on cue, Rankin's car suddenly sped up and roared through a yellow light, then turned south again. Brady floored the accelerator and swerved out of the traffic, mounting the sidewalk in a hopeless attempt to keep up with him.

The light turned red just as Brady flew through the intersection.

Another car broadsided him.

Brady smashed his head on the steering wheel, and everything went dark.

## 11.01 am: Intersection of Vine and Port streets.

Brady woke with a start and tried to move.

His seatbelt stopped him. And his fucking head. He felt like he had the worst hangover of his life.

From somewhere he heard a voice. "Are you okay mister?"

Brady blinked to clear his vision. When that didn't work he squeezed his eyes shut and opened them again. Outside his window, a crowd of people was rubbernecking around his car.

Steam rose from beneath the bonnet.

He looked around, as if he was in a dream.

"What the fuck?"

A man with bright white teeth and too much product in his hair reached through the car window and grabbed Brady's shoulder reassuringly.

"You were in an accident. Don't move. An ambulance is on its way."

Brady looked around groggily and tried to get his bearings.

His head beat like an angry drum. When he touched it he saw blood on his fingers.

A woman with blonde curly hair started screaming at him. "You were driving like a maniac. You could have killed someone."

The haze cleared like a fog on a sunny day. Brady grabbed the wheel and sat up in the driver's seat.

The Monster.

He was chasing the Monster.

"How long was I out?"

The man with the white teeth spoke to him like a child. "A few minutes. You need to relax, okay. The ambulance is on its way."

Brady shrugged off his hand and swore loudly as he tried to turn over the ignition.

The car whined, chugged, then died.

Brady undid his seatbelt and tried to get out of the car, but he couldn't, instead he staggered and fell back in the seat.

The world spun and dipped like a roundabout.

"Hey, what are you doing?" the angry woman screeched. "You can't leave the scene of an accident! The police are coming."

Brady straightened up and pulled his badge from his belt, holding it up so they all could see.

"I am the police. Now move out of the fucking way."

Brady turned the ignition again and there was nothing. He tried again and again and then the car sputtered to life. He slammed the door, revved the engine, and dropped it into gear, pulling away from the wreck and speeding south towards Meadow Avenue.

## 11.25 am: 108 Meadow Avenue.

Brady pulled up a block from Doreen Hansen's house.

The car whined and sputtered like an old smoker with emphysema as it came to a stop. The whole street could probably hear him coming. Brady opened the door and got out, gingerly testing his balance. His head was pounding and every now and then his vision was nothing more than a blur.

He was pretty sure he had a concussion.

Brady looked up and down the street before making his way to 108.

It was empty. Rankin's Ford was nowhere to be seen.

When he reached the house Brady drew his revolver and started slowly up drive. The white pebbles crunched beneath his feet. He licked his lips anxiously and crossed the yard towards the front steps, mindful of movement at the windows.

They looked dark and silent.

A strong gust of wind rose up across the yard, sending brown leaves tumbling through the grass and a chill down Brady's spine.

He climbed the front steps one by one by one, careful not to make a sound. When he reached the top, he crossed the porch and stood to listen at the front door.

He could hear muffled music.

Voices maybe?

Gently, Brady wrapped his hand around the doorknob and turned. It was locked. He couldn't get inside that way. He was going to have to go around the back. Brady gripped his pistol tight and breathed deeply, trying to keep his focus.

His head pounded and his vision was blurry.

Slowly, Brady made his way around to the side of the house. He opened a tall, mission-brown wooden gate that led to the back yard. It squeaked loudly as it opened and Brady froze, listening intently for any movement.

But there was nothing.

Not even the dog.

He swallowed hard over the lump in his throat and crept on, stopping at the corner to peer into the yard.

It was engulfed in a tangle of overgrown grass and weeds. A rusted swing sat in the back corner near an old tumbledown breezeblock barbecue. Brady scanned the yard, checking for movement, then started slowly towards the back porch.

The old lady's dog was asleep, lying beneath a picnic table on the crumbling patio.

He had to keep it calm. If it started barking, Rankin would know he was here.

Brady moved closer to the sleeping dog.

"Sssh..." he whispered. "Who's a good dog?"

The dog didn't move.

He stepped closer and reached out his hand.

Nothing.

Brady took another step forward. The dog wasn't asleep. It was lying in a pool of blood, its head cleaved open in a mess of fur and brains.

"Jesus fucking Christ," he said, too loudly.

Brady looked around, checking no one had heard him.

He was alone. Ahead was a sliding door that led into the house.

He could feel his balls retract in fear. He didn't want to go in there. No one would ever want to go in there. Brady crept towards the door; he could hear the rush of blood from his heart in his ears.

His breathing was shallow and laboured, and his hands were shaking. His vision swirled before him.

He had to keep calm.

He had to hold it together.

Brady tested the sliding door and it opened. He took a deep breath to steel his nerves, then pulled back the curtains and slipped inside.

Loud rock music and the stench of death assaulted him.

He was in the kitchen. It looked empty. Cautiously, he took another step into the dark. Every countertop was filled with garbage. Flies hovered around dirty plates and refuse was stacked high in the sink and on the kitchen table.

The tap dripped intermittently.

He took a step forward, then another. Suddenly a rat jumped out from the filth and screeched. Startled, Brady pointed his gun in fright as it scurried off into the shadows.

His heart thundered and his hands shook with fear.

Muffled rock music came from somewhere.

Brady could see the light from the next room up ahead and he slowly crossed the kitchen into the living room, his gun drawn and finger on the trigger.

He peered inside.

Most of the room was a shadowy maze of waist-high junk and magazines. In the middle of it all was a couch and a TV. Two figures sat on the couch, staring ahead blankly, the white static of the dead channel jumping and shifting like a strobe light in the darkness.

Brady levelled his gun at the people on the couch.

"Police!" he yelled. "Don't you fucking move."

Neither of them moved.

Brady circled around slowly, keeping the gun trained on them.

They figures sat motionless, watching the snow on the screen as if he wasn't there. As he moved around in front of them, he could see their faces...

They looked like dolls.

Lifelike dolls...

There were two bodies. One was Doreen Hansen, dead, her eyes open wide and staring at the TV, her throat slashed from ear to ear. The figure next to her was the mummified body of a young girl, her blonde hair falling over her shoulders. She was dressed in a pink Victorian-style frock; her skin was tanned the colour of a brown leather bag.

The girl's eyes, mouth and ears were sewn shut.

Brady did his best to stifle a scream. He started hyperventilating, his hands shaking so much he almost dropped his gun.

"This can't be real..." he moaned to himself. "None of this is real..."

He felt as though he was watching himself, just like he was in the audience at a cinema watching a fucking house of horrors flick...

He could feel his sanity start to slip away as terror gripped him like never before in his life. He wanted to run away. He needed a drink so badly. But he couldn't. He had to find Abby before it was too late. He did his best to pull himself together.

Where the fuck could she be?

The sound of music from downstairs.

The old woman said she heard people in her basement.

Brady slowly crossed the room to the basement door, his eyes wide and large like an owl's, his head snapping left and right at the slightest movement.

Brady felt he was going to be sick, and he was having trouble keeping his eyes in focus.

As soon as he pulled the door open, deafening music blared. It was the same song on repeat. Brady kept his eyes on the gloom of the stairwell and felt around for a light switch. When he found it, he flicked it on. Nothing. He flicked it off and tried again. Nothing. There was no bulb in the fixture overhead and the only light came from the room behind him and the basement below.

Brady gripped the rickety railing tight and started down the stairs. The wooden steps groaned underfoot, and Brady kept his gun aimed towards the bottom, finger poised over the trigger.

It felt cold down there, damp.

There was something else as well, a feeling almost impossible to describe, as if every molecule of this place was defiled by the fear and agony and brutality that inhabited it.

Brady reached the bottom of the stairs and slowly moved out into the basement. Shadows criss-crossed the space. The ceiling above was low, almost claustrophobic, and it felt as if the room was pressing in on every side. Within the shadows Brady could see dilapidated furniture and rows of floor-to-ceiling shelves crowded with jars and toys and tools and junk. He moved further into the basement, past the rows of shelves.

The light grew brighter.

His head still felt woozy, and panic gripped his chest so tightly he could barely breathe...

The basement opened out into a wide room. And then he saw her.

Abby Robbins was cuffed by her feet and hands to a ring on the floor. Her mouth was gagged and wrapped in duct tape. She was moaning and when she saw Brady she started struggling like a trapped animal.

Behind her was a small table with an 8mm projector. It was playing a grainy film on the wall. At first Brady thought what he was seeing was a fake, a movie of some kind. But it wasn't. It was real.

It was Joseph King being tortured and killed.

Brady's heart pounded like it would burst as he ran over to Abby's side, holstering his gun.

"It's okay," he said, speaking as softly as he could over the loud music. "I'm a police officer. I'm here to help you."

Abby screamed through her gag and cowered like a frightened animal. Her hands were covered in blood from where her finger had been bitten off, her wrists and ankles were raw meat from trying to break free.

He could see the absolute terror in her eyes.

"It's alright. Please, let me help you," Brady said, reaching for her hand.

She flinched at his touch.

"I'm not going to hurt you. I'm gonna get you out of here, I promise."

Brady tried to touch her shoulder.

This time she stopped screaming and let him.

"It alright," Brady said, doing his best to keep the girl calm. "He can't hurt you now."

Her eyes grew wide and terrified and she started screaming again, her entire body straining against the cuffs.

"I'm gonna get you out of here," Brady said, ripping the tape from her lips.

Her mouth was stuffed with rags.

"It's okay. You're okay. I just need to know where he is. Where's the man who kidnapped you?"

Brady pulled the last of the rags from Abby's mouth. She gasped desperately for air and started sobbing uncontrollably.

"He's right behind you."

Her words sent a shock wave through Brady's body. As he turned, the Monster emerged from the shadows on the far side of the room into the light, naked and insane, a knife in one hand, a cleaver in the other.

It was Ted Rankin, but it wasn't him anymore. His eyes

were dark, bottomless pits, his face cracked with a deranged and evil grin. The man before them was a maniac, pure and simple, a killer devoid of human emotion, feeling or sentiment.

The Monster stopped before them and stood motionless, watching, regarding them both, drinking in their fear.

Brady got to his feet slowly, careful not to make a sudden move, and put himself between the Monster and Abby. Fear coursed through his body.

The Monster neither said nor did a thing.

"Put down the knives, Ted," Brady said as calmly as he could. "You don't want to do this, alright?"

The Monster stared at him.

"You need help man... you're sick..." Brady's voice broke and trembled. "I'll get you some help, just please put down the weapons and this will all be over."

"Do you want to know what pain is?" the Monster asked menacingly.

Brady could feel the charge in the air.

"Please Ted, let me help you. You don't wanna do this... you don't wanna hurt this girl, do you?"

"DO YOU WANT TO KNOW WHAT PAIN IS?" the Monster screamed and started across the basement towards Brady and Abby, cleaver raised over his head, ready to strike.

Abby screamed and Brady dropped to one knee, quickly

drawing his weapon from its holster and taking aim.

It happened in a split second.

Gunshots rang out.

The muzzle flash of the revolver lit up the room, one, two, three. The Monster stopped in his tracks as two gunshots exploded in his neck. He dropped the knife and the cleaver almost immediately and clawed at his throat, gurgling, struggling to breathe.

He fell to his knees, then on his side and spasmed on the floor. Then he was still. The Monster was dead.

Brady sat on the basement floor and wrapped his arms around the screaming girl, cradling her like a baby.

She was safe.

The Monster couldn't hurt her anymore.

**2.10 pm: 108 Meadow Avenue.**

Brady stood next to Captain Dodd, watching as Abby Robbins was stretchered out of the house. Her parents stood by her on either side, doting, telling her everything was going to be alright.

Brady smiled at this.

It might be the first time he'd been happy since his wife left him.

"You did good here today, Brady," Dodd said. "No one would have figured that out. Not in a million years."

"Yeah, well, I got lucky."

Dodd squeezed Brady's shoulder.

"Look, I know you've had a tough couple of weeks but with this arrest, I'm sure I can get you reinstated and have those charges against you dropped."

Brady lit a cigarette.

"I appreciate everything you've done for me, Captain. I really do. But I'm giving my notice and I'm gonna plead guilty to the charges. I don't want to be a cop anymore. I should have figured that out a long time ago."

Brady parked outside his old house and walked up to the front door, knocked softly and waited for his wife to answer.

"You stood me up the cafe today," Heidi scowled as she opened the door.

"Yeah, I'm sorry. I couldn't help it."

She folded her arms across her chest, but for once she didn't seem angry. "I saw you on the news. Are you okay?"

"Yeah, I'm okay. Look, I don't want to fight anymore..."

Her eyes narrowed and her demeanour soured. "Brady, this isn't up for discussion. I want a divorce."

"Yeah, I know you do. I'm here to sign the papers. Whatever you want."

"Are you serious?"

Brady nodded.

"You're right to be angry at me and I'm sorry. But that's not going to change what I've done to you or Ellie or our family. I know that now. I know I can never make that right or get you both back. And I'm not asking you to forgive me. I'm just asking you to understand that I'm sorry.

"You tell your lawyer to send through the papers and I'll sign whatever they are, I'll agree to whatever custody arrangement you want. Truth is, I'm going to go to jail for a long time. We all know I was a shitty husband and an even shitter father. So, you and Ellie should move on. Maybe one day, if I'm lucky, Ellie will let me be in her life again."

Tears welled in Heidi's eyes, but she didn't say a word. Brady smiled at this, and she let him kiss her on the cheek.

He turned to leave, then stopped.

"About Neil... I never told you."

She looked at him like her heart was about to break.

He wanted to tell her about that day, about what really happened to their son. He wanted to tell her that he'd put Neil in the bath then gone and left him alone, had a beer or two and watched the end of the game. He wanted to tell her that time got away from him and when he remembered he ran back into the bathroom to find their little boy dead at the bottom of the bathtub.

He wanted to tell her that it was all his fault.

That he killed their son and if he had been there looking after him like he was supposed to, Neil would be here right now, they'd all be together and none of this would ever have happened.

But he couldn't. He couldn't even admit to himself.

What was it going to change if he told her the truth? Was it going to ease her suffering? Was it going to make her life better knowing that her son died because her husband was a selfish, negligent fuck who cared more about watching a game of football that their son's life?

He'd unburden himself to her and open old wounds that were

never going to heal right anyway, except now there'd be a whole new layer of pain to them.

All the truth would do was ease his own suffering.

And he deserved to suffer.

"What about him?" Heidi asked.

"Nothing..." Brady said trying to talk over the lump in his throat. "I guess I never told you how much I miss him."

**8.16 pm: Brady Hitchcock's apartment.**

He sat on his couch, an open bottle of vodka on the coffee table before him.

After Brady had said goodbye to his wife, he drove to the hospital and sat by John Bailey's bedside.

He was in a vegetative state and probably would never wake up from the beating Brady had given him. He shouldn't have done that. Brady always knew he was wrong. He had told himself that the rage and the drugs took over and made him do something he wouldn't normally do.

But the truth was, he was an angry person.

A horrible man with no control over himself or his emotions.

Admitting that didn't change anything. And sitting next to John Bailey, watching a machine breathe for him, all of his apologies felt empty. No one was there to hear them. The day Brady had bashed this man with a wheel brace till he was almost dead, he robbed him of the chance of vindication and justice.

It was all the more tragic because, in a couple of hours, Bailey's son was about to turn himself in as the driver who hit that girl.

All of it was for nothing.

Brady sat in his living room and drank deeply from the bottle of vodka. He opened the one photo album Heidi had given him in the breakup. It was of a trip they took with Heidi's sister to a lake. Ellie was young in the pictures, no more than four years old. He remembered the day so clearly because there were swans at the lake, and they were nesting. At one point, one of the birds had charged at Ellie when she got too close to its eggs and Brady had protected her.

It was one of his favourite memories.

It always made him feel like a great dad. But he knew it hadn't turned out that way. Ellie wouldn't even speak to him anymore. His daughter didn't even want to know him anymore.

And his son... his little boy.

He'd let everyone down.

And now he was alone.

He turned the page in the album. Maybe none of this ever even happened, maybe he simply wasn't there, just a delusion along with everything else.

Maybe he'd wake up and it'd be that day, back at the lake. Or the day Neil died.

Maybe he'd get a chance to make all of his mistakes right and he'd wake up and these last few years had been a dream, some kind of horrible nightmare, and Heidi and Ellie and Neil would all be there, and everything would be alright.

Brady retrieved his little brown leather kit from beneath the couch and cooked up a shot of heroin. Maybe he'd get one more chance to make it right. Like he had with Abby Robbins. He'd saved her from the Monster. But wasn't he one too?

Was this eternal return?

When he saved Abby, did he save himself as well? Or was all this just a jumble of memories he could no longer make sense of anymore? Was it a test that he needed to pass, or was he simply clutching at random memories tumbling from his broken mind?

Brady pressed the needle into his vein and gasped as he pushed down on the stopper. A rush rumbled through in his heart, and he fell to the carpet.

He gasped once, then twice... it seemed that time no longer mattered, that nothing else mattered. He could hear his loved ones calling to him from across the ages. Their voices were heavenly, and they made his very soul feel as it might burst with joy and happiness. And loudest of them all was his son Neil, beckoning to him to join them, calling for his father to finally come home.

Maybe Brady would wake up tomorrow and he'd know the answer to eternal return... or maybe, just maybe, he'd never wake again.

THE END.